ECHOS OF JUSTICE

The Cassie Chronicles

Demantaze Moore

Copyright © 2024 Demantaze Moore

All rights reserved

The characters and events portrayed in this book are fictitious. Any similarity to real persons, living or dead, is coincidental and not intended by the author.

No part of this book may be reproduced, or stored in a retrieval system, or transmitted in any form or by any means, electronic, mechanical, photocopying, recording, or otherwise, without express written permission of the publisher.

Cover design by: Demantaze Moore
Printed in the United States of America

"In the shadows, justice finds its voice, whispering the truths that echo through the silence of deceit."

DEDICATION

To the unsung heroes of law enforcement and intelligence agencies worldwide, who risk their lives daily to protect us from the shadows. Your courage, dedication, and unwavering commitment to justice inspire this story.

This book is a small testament to your tireless efforts, your sacrifices, and your unwavering pursuit of truth in a world often shrouded in darkness. Your work is not always seen, but it is profoundly felt. May this story serve as a reminder of the constant battle against those who seek to undermine peace and security, and the brave individuals who stand against them.

This is dedicated to you, the silent guardians, the protectors in the night, those who embody the true meaning of resilience, loyalty, and unwavering pursuit of justice. May this narrative capture even a fraction of the grit, determination, and moral compass that guides your extraordinary work, a work that makes the world a safer, more just place, one case at a time. Your service is invaluable, and your dedication never goes unnoticed.

PREFACE

Every journey begins with a single step, and every story with a single idea. This book is the culmination of countless hours of thought, research, and personal experience. It is a reflection of the complexities of our world, where the line between right and wrong is often blurred, and where courage and determination are required to navigate the shadows.

My time in the Army, particularly my years in military intelligence and providing convoy security, has deeply influenced the narrative within these pages. The experiences I encountered, the people I met, and the challenges I faced have all left an indelible mark on my perspective. This story is not just a work of fiction, but a testament to the resilience and tenacity of those who serve, both in the military and in the security industry.

I have endeavored to craft a tale that is both thrilling and thought-provoking. The characters, though products of my imagination, carry the weight of real-world dilemmas and moral quandaries. Their journeys mirror the struggle to find justice in a world fraught with deception and danger.

As you embark on this journey with Cassie, Benjamin, and Dimitri, I hope you find yourself drawn into the intricate web of intrigue and suspense. May their trials and triumphs resonate with you, and may you find inspiration in their unwavering pursuit of truth.

Thank you for joining me on this adventure. Your support and engagement are what bring these stories to life.

With gratitude, Demantaze Moore

INTRODUCTION

The journey to creating "Echoes of Justice: The Cassie Chronicles" has been a remarkable and deeply personal experience. This book is more than a work of fiction; it is a tribute to the resilience, courage, and unwavering dedication of those who serve in the shadows, often unseen but always vigilant.

My background in the Army, particularly my years in military intelligence and providing convoy security, has profoundly influenced the themes and characters within these pages. The complexities of duty, the weight of responsibility, and the relentless pursuit of justice are threads that weave through this narrative, drawn from real-life experiences and the extraordinary people I have had the privilege to know.

In crafting this story, I aimed to explore the human spirit's depth and the bonds forged in the crucible of shared adversity. Cassie, Benjamin, and Dimitri are embodiments of the strength, intelligence, and tenacity required to navigate a world fraught with deception and danger. Their journey is a testament to the power of trust and the unyielding resolve to seek justice, no matter the cost.

To my readers, thank you for embarking on this adventure with me. Your support and engagement bring these characters to life, and your curiosity drives the exploration of the intricate webs of intrigue and suspense. I hope this story resonates with you, offering not only entertainment but also a reflection on the values and sacrifices that define true heroism.

With gratitude, Demantaze Moore

PROLOGUE

The room was cloaked in darkness, the only light emanating from the flickering screen of a laptop. Cassie Holloway sat motionless, her gaze fixed on the data scrolling before her. Each piece of information was a puzzle piece, each clue a fragment of a larger, more sinister picture. The conspiracy she had uncovered was vast, its tendrils reaching into the highest echelons of power and influence.

Cassie's mind was a whirlwind of thoughts, each one more unsettling than the last. The mission in Monaco had been a success, but at a terrible cost. The faces of those lost haunted her, their sacrifices a constant reminder of the price of justice. Beside her, Benjamin and his twin brother Dimitri shared her burden, their silent presence a testament to their unyielding commitment to the cause.

Dimitri, with his military precision and unflinching resolve, had been instrumental in their success. His tactical expertise and unwavering loyalty had saved them more than once. Yet, even his formidable skills were tested by the shadowy network they faced. The enemy was cunning, their operations shrouded in secrecy, their motives as elusive as smoke.

Benjamin, ever the detective, had spent countless hours poring over the evidence, piecing together the intricate web of deceit and betrayal. His sharp mind and meticulous attention to detail had uncovered connections others had missed, revealing the true scale of the threat they faced. Yet, despite their progress, the path ahead remained fraught with danger.

As Cassie, Benjamin, and Dimitri prepared to delve deeper into the conspiracy, they knew their journey was far from over. The echoes of justice called to them, urging them forward, their resolve strengthened by the bond they shared. Together, they would face the darkness, uncover the truth, and bring those responsible to justice.

The battle had just begun.

ECHOES OF JUSTICE: THE CASSIE CHRONICLES

CHAPTER 1

The Initial Breach

"The air hung thick with the metallic tang of fear, the acrid bite of rain lashing against the Shard's glass facade - a prelude to the chaos that had just begun."

The air hung thick with the metallic tang of fear and the acrid bite of rain lashing against the glass facade of the Shard's annex. Sirens wailed a mournful counterpoint to the frantic shouts echoing from within. Cassie Reynolds, her tailored suit a stark contrast to the chaos unfolding around her, surveyed the scene with the cold precision of a surgeon preparing for a complex operation. Her dark eyes, usually sparkling with an almost mischievous intelligence, were narrowed, assessing the scene with clinical detachment. This wasn't a simple hostage situation; the air thrummed with something far more sinister.

The annex, normally a gleaming showcase of modern architecture, was now a grim tableau of police tape and anxious faces. A phalanx of armed officers, their expressions grim and determined, formed a perimeter, their weapons trained on the building's entrance. From her vantage point, Cassie could see the flickering emergency lights casting an eerie glow on the rain-slicked streets. The scene pulsed with an energy that was both terrifying and exhilarating, the kind of pressure that both thrilled and terrified her. She was in her element, the adrenaline a familiar companion.

This wasn't her first rodeo. Cassie had negotiated her way through countless hostage crises across the globe, each one a perilous dance on the edge of catastrophe. Yet, something about this felt different. The initial communications with the hostage-takers, relayed through a crackling police radio, were curt, devoid of the usual frantic demands for ransom or media attention. There was a chilling calculation in their silence, a carefully constructed coldness that sent shivers down her spine. It felt…orchestrated.

Detective Inspector Benjamin Moore, a man whose cynicism was only surpassed by his sharp intellect, stood beside her, observing with a mixture of skepticism and grudging respect. He was a creature of habit, preferring the methodical process of investigation to the high-wire act of negotiation. His presence, however, was a testament to the gravity of the situation. Benjamin, a man who rarely displayed emotion, watched Cassie with a level of intense scrutiny that bordered on obsession.

"They're not asking for money, Reynolds," Benjamin stated, his voice low and gravelly, cutting through the background noise. He was a man whose words were as precisely honed as the blade of a scalpel. "Not yet, anyway. This isn't your typical grab-and-run. Something else is going on here."

Cassie nodded, her gaze fixed on the building. "I agree. The lack of demands is…unusual. It suggests a more elaborate agenda. They're playing a longer game." Her fingers, usually nimble and quick, traced the outline of a barely perceptible scratch on the glass of her watch, a nervous habit she couldn't seem to shake.

The initial attempts at communication were frustratingly

unproductive. The hostage-takers responded in short, clipped sentences, their voices heavily disguised. They refused to identify themselves or state their demands, only offering cryptic pronouncements that seemed designed to confuse and unsettle. Their words, delivered with a chilling calm, spoke of a larger plan, a calculated strategy that went far beyond the immediate hostage crisis. It was a chess game, and Cassie suspected she was only seeing a few carefully placed pieces on the board.

As the hours ticked by, the tension in the air thickened. The initial optimism of a swift resolution had evaporated, replaced by a creeping sense of dread. Cassie's usually unflappable demeanor began to crack under the weight of the situation. She sensed a deliberate delay, a calculated stalling tactic, designed to buy time for something…else.

The initial phase of the negotiation was a tense stand-off, a battle of wits played out in the shadows of the towering building. Cassie tried every tactic in her arsenal – empathy, reasoned argument, even calculated threats – but each attempt was met with the same chilling indifference. Her calm exterior was a carefully constructed façade, masking a growing unease that gnawed at her confidence. She was out of her depth, facing an enemy as elusive and unpredictable as the shifting tides of the Thames.

Benjamin, initially skeptical of Cassie's methods, started to see a glimmer of her genius. Her intuition, sharpened by years of experience, allowed her to recognize subtle cues, minute details that others would have overlooked. He began to appreciate her ability to anticipate the next move of her adversaries, a skill honed through countless high-stakes encounters.

Then came the critical error. A lapse in judgment, a moment of misplaced trust, a crucial detail overlooked in the relentless pressure of the situation. It happened quickly, a seemingly innocuous decision that unleashed a cascade of unforeseen consequences. One of the hostages, a young woman, made a sudden, unexpected move, triggering a violent response from the hostage-takers. The situation spiralled out of control, escalating into a chaotic and violent struggle. The carefully constructed facade of calm shattered, plunging the operation into a desperate, life-or-death struggle.

The scene descended into a maelstrom of gunfire and screams, the carefully orchestrated dance of negotiation replaced by a brutal ballet of survival. The initial calmness was shattered, replaced by the desperate urgency of the moment. The hostage-takers, initially elusive and cryptic, had revealed their true nature – ruthless, violent, and utterly unpredictable.

The initial breach had become a full-blown crisis, demanding immediate and decisive action. Cassie and Benjamin, forced into an uneasy alliance by the unfolding chaos, knew that their skills, their experience, and their very lives, were on the line. They had to work together, to navigate the treacherous path ahead, if they hoped to survive the night. The line between success and catastrophic failure was now razor thin. The unexpected alliance, born of necessity, was the only thing standing between them and oblivion. The game had begun.

CHAPTER 2

Unexpected Alliance

"Their uneasy alliance, forged in the crucible of chaos, became a necessity, a lifeline in the face of an escalating crisis."

The shattered glass crunched underfoot, a grim soundtrack to the chaos that still reigned. The initial assault had left a trail of destruction – overturned furniture, shattered display cases, and the lingering smell of cordite mingling with the rain-soaked air. Cassie, her breath ragged but her focus unwavering, assessed the damage. Two hostages lay injured, their screams now muted by the arrival of paramedics. The hostage-takers, three figures shrouded in shadows, had vanished into the labyrinthine corridors of the annex. Benjamin Moore, his usually sharp features etched with grim determination, moved with the practiced efficiency of a man who'd seen too much death. He barked orders at the arriving SWAT team, his voice cutting through the cacophony. His methodical approach was a stark contrast to Cassie's more improvisational style, a difference that was already proving to be a source of friction in their unplanned partnership. "They're professionals," Benjamin stated, his gaze sweeping over the scene. "This wasn't a random act. Too clean, too coordinated."

Cassie, crouching beside one of the injured hostages, carefully examined a small, almost imperceptible scratch on the victim's arm. "You think it's something bigger?" she asked, her voice low. The scratch, barely visible, seemed insignificant, yet to her trained eye, it spoke volumes. "Bigger than a simple bank robbery? Definitely," Benjamin replied, his eyes narrowing. He gestured towards a partially destroyed security camera. "Look at this. They knew exactly where the blind spots were. They knew the building's layout better than the security detail."

Cassie straightened, the implications hitting her with the force of a physical blow. This wasn't a simple hostage situation. This was a meticulously planned operation, a precision strike designed to create a distraction. But a distraction from what?

The answer came in the form of a frantic call from DI Evans, Benjamin's superior. Evans' voice was strained, laced with a desperation that mirrored the rising panic in Cassie's own heart. "Moore, Reynolds," he gasped, "we've just received intelligence. There's a secondary target. A shipment of…something… is being transported across the Thames. The hostage situation… it's a diversion."

The pieces began to fall into place. The meticulously planned attack, the precision of the hostage-takers' movements, the almost surgical efficiency of their escape – it all pointed towards a larger, more sinister plot. The hostage crisis was a smokescreen, a carefully orchestrated distraction to mask a far greater threat.

Their uneasy alliance, forged in the crucible of chaos, became a necessity, a lifeline in the face of an escalating crisis. Their contrasting styles clashed. Benjamin, a stickler for protocol and procedure, found Cassie's intuitive approach to negotiation infuriatingly unpredictable. Cassie, in turn, chafed under Benjamin's rigid adherence to rules, his reluctance to deviate from the established plan. "We need to get to that shipment," Cassie stated, her voice firm despite the fatigue that gnawed at her. "We have to intercept it before they get away."

Benjamin's skepticism was evident. "We're talking about a high-risk operation. We're outnumbered, outgunned. Jumping into another potentially lethal situation without proper backup is reckless." "We don't have the luxury of time, Moore," Cassie retorted, her patience wearing thin. The adrenaline coursing through her veins fueled her resolve. "This is bigger than either of us. It's about national security."

Their argument was interrupted by a sudden flurry of gunfire echoing from a nearby alleyway. Instinctively, Cassie shoved Benjamin behind a wrecked car, her training kicking in. They were ambushed. A hail of bullets ripped through the air, narrowly missing them.

Cassie, using her surroundings to her advantage, returned fire with surprising accuracy, drawing on her years of experience in handling high-pressure situations. Her quick thinking, her ability to assess the situation and respond decisively, saved them both. Benjamin, initially stunned by the ferocity of the attack, found himself relying on Cassie's instincts. He provided cover, his firearm a steady stream of controlled bursts, while Cassie moved them to a more defensible position.

The ambush was short-lived. The attackers, apparently surprised by Cassie's unexpected counterattack, retreated. The silence that followed was heavy, punctuated only by the distant sirens.

In the aftermath of the attack, a grudging respect began to bloom between them. Benjamin, witnessing Cassie's resourcefulness and courage firsthand, saw a level of expertise beyond his expectations. Cassie, observing Benjamin's tactical prowess and his ability to maintain order amidst chaos, acknowledged his skill and experience. Their shared goal – to stop the larger threat – superseded their differences, their contrasting personalities forging an unusual but increasingly effective partnership.

Their next move required a degree of subterfuge. Information gleaned from a wounded attacker, coupled with Cassie's analysis of the initial attack and the cryptic messages left by the hostage-takers, led them to a seemingly innocuous warehouse on the docks. The shipment, they suspected, was headed there.

The warehouse was a maze of shadows and steel, a silent monument to industrial decay. They moved with caution, Benjamin leading the way, his keen senses alert for any sign of danger. Cassie, her eyes constantly scanning for anything out of place, played the role of the cautious observer, ensuring their every move was calculated and deliberate. Their contrasting approaches, once a source of friction, now worked in perfect harmony, a deadly dance of precision and intuition.

The warehouse's interior was shrouded in darkness, broken only by the occasional flicker of a distant light. The air hung heavy with the scent of machinery oil and damp concrete. The sounds of their footsteps echoed through the cavernous space, each sound a potential alert to the enemy.

As they crept deeper into the warehouse, they stumbled upon the heart of the operation – a large container truck, its doors sealed tight. The air around the truck hummed with a strange energy, a faint vibration that spoke of something clandestine and powerful. They didn't know exactly what was inside, but they knew one thing – this was the culmination of their pursuit, the apex of the crisis.

Suddenly, the warehouse doors burst open. More assailants flooded the scene, their weapons raised. This was no simple shipment; it was a carefully planned ambush, meant to eliminate them. The fight was on, a desperate struggle for survival in the echoing darkness of the warehouse. The unexpected alliance between the negotiator and the detective, once born of necessity, had become a powerful force, a beacon of hope against the encroaching darkness. The game was far from over; it had only just begun its most dangerous chapter.

CHAPTER 3

Introduction of the Twin Brother

"The combined expertise of the three—Cassie's negotiation skills, Benjamin's detective work, and Dimitri's military background—proved invaluable. But the clock was ticking, and failure was not an option."

The warehouse doors, previously a gaping maw spewing chaos, now stood relatively still, the frantic rush of assailants replaced by a tense silence. The air hung thick with the metallic tang of blood and the acrid bite of gunpowder. Cassie, her hands still trembling slightly, checked the pulse of a young woman clutching a shredded handbag. The paramedic, efficient and grim-faced, nodded grimly. Stable, for now.

Benjamin, meanwhile, moved through the wreckage, his sharp gaze missing nothing. He registered the type of weaponry used – sophisticated, military-grade – the precision of the attack, the almost surgical removal of the initial hostage-takers. This wasn't a random act of violence; it was orchestrated, calculated, and terrifyingly efficient. He found his partner, Detective Inspector Ava Sharma, her face smudged with grime and sweat, but her eyes burning with a controlled fury. "Anything?" she rasped, her voice hoarse from shouting orders.

"It's bigger than we thought," Benjamin replied, his voice low. "Military-grade equipment, coordinated assault… this is beyond a simple robbery."

Just then, a figure emerged from the shadows. Tall, powerfully built, with the quiet intensity that only years of rigorous training could forge. He wore a simple black tactical vest over a dark shirt, his face etched with the kind of controlled weariness that spoke of countless sleepless nights and high-stakes missions. This was Dimitri Moore, Benjamin's twin brother, a Navy SEAL with a reputation that preceded him.

The reunion was silent, a brief exchange of glances that spoke volumes. Benjamin, the reserved detective, and Dimiti the stoic warrior, shared a bond forged in shared childhoods and honed by years of unspoken understanding.

"Dimitri," Benjamin breathed, relief and a touch of something else – perhaps guilt – coloring his voice. "What are you doing here?"

"I received a call," Dimitri responded, his voice a low rumble, devoid of unnecessary pleasantries. "My intel suggests this goes deeper than a simple hostage situation.
Much deeper."

He produced a small, encrypted device, its screen glowing faintly. "This was intercepted. It's a fragmented communication, but it indicates a connection to a clandestine operation I've been tracking – codenamed 'Project Nightingale'."

Cassie, who had been observing the exchange with keen interest, stepped forward. "Project Nightingale?" she asked, her voice professional, concealing her rising apprehension. "We haven't encountered anything like that in our briefing."

Dimitri nodded, handing the device to Benjamin. "It involves a network of operatives, a highly sophisticated arms deal, and... possibly a bioweapon." The revelation sent a chill down Cassie's spine. Bioweapon? This escalated the stakes exponentially. Her experience with hostage negotiations was extensive, but this was a whole new level of threat. The scale of this operation dwarfed anything she had encountered before.

Benjamin, meanwhile, was already analyzing the encrypted data on the device. His skill in decryption was formidable; he could see the faint digital fingerprints, the hidden layers of code attempting to mask the true content.

Dimitri, however, saw the situation from a tactical, military perspective. His years in the Navy SEALs had trained him to anticipate threats, assess vulnerabilities, and strategize for maximum impact. He saw the pattern, a strategic chess game played by highly trained individuals.

The combined expertise of the three—Cassie's negotiation skills, Benjamin's detective work, and Dimitri's military background—proved invaluable. They began piecing together the fragments of information, each adding a new layer to the intricate puzzle. Dimitri's military contacts proved helpful, leading them to a network of shadowy figures operating in the underworld of international espionage.

Benjamin used his contacts within Scotland Yard to piece together the fragmented trail left by the hostage-takers. Cassie, with her skill in interpreting human behavior and her intimate knowledge of negotiating tactics, offered insight into the hostage-takers' motivations, a deeper understanding of their thought processes that even Benjamin and Dimitri couldn't fathom.

The fragmented communication mentioned a series of coded messages hidden within seemingly innocuous online forums.

Dimitri, familiar with such methods of covert communication, quickly deciphered the codes. They
discovered the hostages were not the primary target – they were pawns in a larger game. The real prize, according to their newly gleaned intel, was a revolutionary bioweapon, codenamed 'Seraph', capable of decimating entire populations.

Their investigation led them down a rabbit hole of international intrigue, tracing the hostage-takers to a clandestine organization with ties to several hostile nations. The organization, known only as "The Serpent's Fang," was shrouded in secrecy, its operations extending far beyond the borders of London. They were experts in covert operations and enjoyed the backing of several hostile nations who supplied them with funds, arms, and technology.

As they delved deeper, they discovered that the organization had infiltrated various levels of government, using their influence to protect its operations and obstruct justice. The scope of their conspiracy was breathtaking – a network of corruption spanning continents.

The familial tension between Benjamin and Dimitri, initially subtle, began to surface. Dimitri's methods were direct, decisive, and often ruthless. He was trained to eliminate threats swiftly and efficiently, his approach a stark contrast to Benjamin's more methodical, investigative style. Cassie, caught in the middle, had to navigate the friction between the twins, her role shifting from negotiator to mediator. She had to ensure that their differences didn't derail the mission and ultimately jeopardize the lives of the hostages.

The investigation brought them into contact with a disillusioned former member of The Serpent's Fang, a woman named Anya Petrova. Anya, haunted by her past actions, provided crucial information about the organization's inner workings, including the location of Seraph. The information, however, came with a hefty price –Anya's life was now in danger, and her cooperation

could
mean the difference between life and death for her and the hostages.

The location Anya revealed was a fortified compound
hidden deep within the Swiss Alps. A seemingly impregnable fortress, protected by state-of-the-art security systems and heavily armed guards, the compound posed a massive challenge. A direct assault was out of the question. Cassie's negotiation skills would be crucial in navigating the treacherous terrain and extracting Seraph, and the hostages, without triggering a violent confrontation that could risk the lives of everyone involved.

The task ahead was daunting, but they knew that failing was not an option. The fate of London, possibly the world, hinged on their success. The uneasy alliance, once a temporary measure, had become a force that could possibly save them all. But the clock was ticking.

CHAPTER 4

Unraveling the Conspiracy

"The true scope of Serpens' ambitions began to unfold, revealing a chilling conspiracy designed to trigger global chaos and reshape the world order. As Cassie and Benjamin stared out over the snow-capped peaks of the Swiss Alps, the weight of their discovery was heavy on their shoulders. Their alliance, forged in crisis, was their best hope against an enemy that seemed as vast and elusive as the mountains before them."

The adrenaline still thrummed in Cassie's veins, a persistent echo of the London chaos. The initial relief at securing the hostages was quickly replaced by a chilling unease. The meticulously planned operation, the precision of the assault, the seemingly random target – it all pointed to something far more sinister than a simple act of terrorism.

Anya, the rescued informant, had whispered fragments of information before collapsing – cryptic phrases, coded messages barely decipherable even by the MI6's best cryptographers. But it was enough to pique Benjamin's interest and confirm Cassie's growing suspicion that this was merely a diversion.

Benjamin, his usually sharp features etched with a grim

determination, was poring over Anya's scattered belongings. He meticulously examined a torn piece of fabric, its intricate weave revealing a hidden emblem – a stylized serpent coiled around a skull, subtly embroidered. The symbol was unfamiliar, yet it resonated with a deep-seated sense of foreboding. He looked up, his gaze meeting Cassie's across the makeshift command center set up in a secure MI6 facility.

"This isn't about ransom," Benjamin stated, his voice low and serious. "This is a distraction."Cassie nodded, her mind racing to connect the disparate pieces of the puzzle. The choice of targets – a seemingly insignificant pharmaceutical company – didn't fit the profile of a typical terrorist organization. The precision of the attack, the level of sophistication employed, hinted at a far more elaborate plan.Their investigation led them down a rabbit hole of encrypted communications, offshore accounts, and shell corporations.

They followed a trail of digital breadcrumbs, tracing the flow of funds and the movement of individuals across
continents. Each lead unravelled another layer of deception, revealing a vast network of seemingly unconnected entities that were all inextricably linked. A breakthrough came in the form of a recovered encrypted hard drive, seized from the warehouse during the raid. The drive contained a series of complex algorithms, painstakingly deciphered by MI6's top cryptographers. The decoded information revealed the existence of "Serpens," a shadowy organization dedicated to global destabilization.

Their modus operandi wasn't brute force, but carefully orchestrated chaos designed to trigger widespread panic and undermine governments. The London hostage crisis, they realized, was just a small, calculated move in a far grander scheme. The symbols, the serpent and skull emblem, appeared repeatedly in the decoded data. It was the Serpens' mark, a branding that spoke of clandestine operations and ruthless efficiency. The organization's goals, as revealed by the documents, were chillingly ambitious – to manipulate global markets, exploit political tensions, and ultimately reshape the world order to their own sinister designs.

The investigation took them from the bustling streets of London to the quiet, cobbled lanes of Geneva, then across the Atlantic to the sun-drenched beaches of Rio. They followed a trail of phantom identities, false flags, and double-crosses, constantly one step behind Serpens' network of operatives. The pursuit was relentless, the stakes
impossibly high. Each step forward brought them closer to the truth, but also into more significant danger. Their alliance, initially forged in the crucible of the London crisis, grew stronger through shared adversity. Benjamin's sharp intellect, his ability to connect seemingly disparate facts, provided the crucial analytical framework. Cassie's negotiation expertise and her calm, strategic thinking helped navigate the treacherous landscape of international intrigue.

The investigation brought them into contact with unexpected allies. A disillusioned former Serpens operative, haunted by his past, offered invaluable information, while a seasoned Interpol agent, skeptical at first, slowly became an essential part of their team. Their network expanded, bringing together individuals from diverse backgrounds – each adding their unique skills and experience to the hunt.

But as they delved deeper into the conspiracy, they faced the chilling realization that Serpens' influence stretched far beyond their initial estimations. The organization had infiltrated various government agencies, multinational corporations, and even powerful financial institutions. Their tentacles extended into the heart of global power structures, making it exceedingly difficult to identify the true leaders and dismantle their network.

The discovery of a secret meeting in a remote location in the Swiss Alps sent a jolt through the investigation team. It was a high-

stakes gamble, but the potential reward was
enormous. If they could infiltrate the meeting, they could possibly expose Serpens' leadership and disrupt their operations.

The alpine compound was a fortress, isolated in the heart of the mountains, protected by high-tech surveillance and heavily armed guards. A direct assault was suicide. Cassie was called upon to use her negotiation skills – not just to extract hostages as before, but to infiltrate the very heart of Serpens' network under false pretenses. Benjamin, while initially hesitant to entrust Cassie to such a dangerous mission, recognized the critical need for her unique skills. He was acutely aware of the inherent risks, the possibility of betrayal, and the devastating consequences of failure. But he also understood the potential payoff –exposure of Serpens, a blow to their operation, and possibly the chance to prevent a catastrophic event that would affect global stability.

Cassie meticulously planned her infiltration. She crafted a false identity, meticulously researched the attendees of the meeting, and learned their routines. She studied their vulnerabilities, their strengths, and their motivations. The plan was daring, bordering on reckless, but the alternative was unthinkable. The infiltration was an exercise in nerve, requiring exceptional control, flawless improvisation, and a considerable dose of luck. Each interaction, each step forward, was laden with peril. Any slip, any moment of doubt, could mean exposure and potentially her life. However, her calm resolve and her ability to read people never faltered.

Her success brought them closer to the center of the organization. The meeting revealed the true scope of Serpens' ambitions, showcasing their meticulously laid plans for global financial chaos. They planned to trigger a series of coordinated events that would cripple the global economy, paving the way for a new world order controlled by them. The information gathered at the summit was invaluable. They now had sufficient evidence to bring down Serpens, atleast those they could identify and locate. But this also brought them to realize that even exposing this vast organization would not destroy them completely. Their roots were deep, their influence pervasive and their reach global. This was only the first step in a long, arduous fight.

The closing moments of the chapter found Cassie and Benjamin staring out over the snow-capped peaks of the Swiss Alps, the weight of their discovery heavy on their shoulders. The victory felt hollow, a fleeting respite in a protracted war against a shadowy enemy. The threat remained, as vast and elusive as the mountain range before them. Their uneasy alliance, forged in the flames of the London hostage crisis, had been tested and proven. The fight had just begun.

CHAPTER 5

First Betrayal

"Betrayal doesn't come with a warning—it arrives silently, with a cold smile and a swift jab. Trust, once shattered, leaves a scar that fuels the relentless pursuit of truth."

The crisp Alpine air did little to soothe the simmering unease that gnawed at Cassie. The breathtaking panorama of snow-capped peaks, usually a source of tranquility, felt like a cold, indifferent witness to the unfolding treachery. Benjamin, ever the pragmatist, was already poring over Anya's fragmented messages, his brow furrowed in concentration. The coded phrases, deciphered partially by MI6's top cryptographers, hinted at a vast conspiracy, a web of deceit that reached far beyond the initial London hostage crisis. "It's not just terrorism, Cassie," Benjamin said, his voice low and gravelly. He looked up from the encrypted data, his eyes reflecting the seriousness of the situation.

"This is… orchestrated. A meticulously planned operation designed to…distract." Cassie nodded, a chill crawling down her spine. The precision of the London attack, the seemingly random target—a mid-level diplomat with minimal security—it all screamed of a calculated distraction. But from what? And who was pulling the strings?

Their investigation led them to a shadowy organization known only as "The Serpent's Tooth," a group rumored to be involved in everything from arms dealing to international assassinations. Their operatives were ghosts, masters of disguise and deception, leaving virtually no trace in their wake. The only lead they had was a name—Anton Volkov—a ruthless operative with a reputation for ruthlessness and unparalleled loyalty to The Serpent's Tooth.

Their next move was to infiltrate a high-stakes auction in Monaco, a known haven for arms dealers and illicit activities. They hoped to use the auction as a cover to gather intelligence, hoping to catch a glimpse of Volkov and glean further information about The Serpent's Tooth. They were aided by a contact, a former MI6 agent named Alistair Finch, who had infiltrated the organization years ago and had remained hidden, quietly gathering intelligence. Finch was their inside man, their key to understanding the organization's inner workings. He'd provided them with logistical support, intelligence, and importantly, a method of blending in.

The auction was a spectacle of opulence and secrecy.Masked figures in expensive suits mingled with equally disguised individuals, their identities shielded behind carefully crafted personas. Cassie and Benjamin, disguised as wealthy art colectors, moved through the crowd, their senses honed for any sign of Volkov or his operatives.

The tension was palpable. Every whispered conversation, every furtive glance, felt charged with a silent threat. The air thrummed with an undercurrent of danger, a palpable sense that they were not alone in their suspicions. As the auction progressed, Cassie felt a prickling sensation at the back of her neck, an instinctive awareness of being watched.

Then came the betrayal. It wasn't a dramatic shootout or a violent confrontation. It was far more subtle, far more insidious. During a brief moment of distraction, while Benjamin was engrossed in observing a suspicious exchange between two masked men, Cassie felt a sharp jab in her side. It was Alistair Finch, her trusted contact, his face devoid of emotion as he injected her with a fast-acting paralytic agent.

Before she succumbed to the drug's effects, she saw Benjamin turn, his expression registering shock and disbelief. Finch, his face a mask of betrayal, simply smiled, a chilling, cold smile that spoke volumes about his true allegiance. The world dissolved into darkness, leaving Cassie with a bitter taste of betrayal and the chilling realization that her trust had been misplaced. The meticulously planned operation, their carefully crafted strategy —all of it had been compromised by a single act of treachery. Benjamin, now alone and facing a far more dangerous situation than he had ever anticipated, was left to grapple with the fallout.

The realization of Finch's double-cross hit him with the force of a physical blow. He had considered Finch an invaluable asset, a lifeline in this treacherous game of cat and mouse with The Serpent's Tooth. The weight of his error pressed down on him, suffocating him. He'd trusted his judgment, trusted Finch, and now his trust had been viciously shattered. The consequences could be catastrophic. He scanned the opulent hall, his mind racing. The security personnel, now alerted to a possible incident, were beginning to converge on Cassie's location. He had to act quickly, decisively. He had to save Cassie and simultaneously find a way to outwit Finch and his employers.

He knew the paralytic agent wouldn't kill her outright, but it would render her completely incapacitated for several hours, enough time for Finch to escape, leaving Benjamin utterly alone against a shadowy force whose reach extended far beyond Monaco. The auction was momentarily thrown into chaos as security rushed to secure Cassie, who lay unconscious on the ornate marble floor. The elegant setting, so recently alive with whispers of clandestine deals and the thrill of bidding wars, now pulsated with fear and confusion. Benjamin, though outwardly calm, felt the panic rising within him. He needed to buy time, to observe Finch's next move. He knew that Finch wouldn't simply vanish. He would leave a trail, however subtle.

He feigned concern for Cassie, expertly playing the role of a distraught art collector, allowing the security personnel to handle the situation while he discreetly observed the room. His keen eyes scanned the crowd, searching for any telltale sign of Finch's escape route, any indication of his next step.

He noticed a subtle change in the dynamics of the room. A group of men, previously inconspicuous amongst the wealthy bidders, were now subtly moving closer to the main exit, their body language suggestive of coordinated action. They were Finch's team, his cleanup crew. Benjamin had to make a split-second decision. He could not confront them directly; outnumbered and outgunned, he would only be captured or killed.

He needed a distraction. With calculated precision, Benjamin subtly triggered the fire alarm. The alarm blared, sending the auction into pandemonium. The chaos provided the perfect cover for his escape. He slipped away unnoticed, amidst the fleeing crowd, his mind already planning his next move.

He had to get to Cassie, to ascertain the nature of the paralytic agent and discover whether it had any long-term effects. More importantly, he needed to uncover the full extent of Finch's betrayal and understand the motivations behind this carefully orchestrated act of treachery.

The adrenaline coursed through his veins, fueling his determination. He wouldn't be defeated. The Serpent's Tooth underestimated him; they underestimated Cassie. Their betrayal had only served to intensify their resolve. The game had changed, but the stakes remained undeniably high. The pursuit of justice, of truth, was now a personal war, a battle fought not only against The Serpent's Tooth but also against the ghosts of shattered trust.

The next phase of their fight had begun, a fight that would test their resilience, their loyalty, and the very foundation of their uneasy alliance to the breaking point. The night was far from over. The first betrayal was merely the prelude to a far greater storm. The question now was, who was next? And who could they trust?

The answer to that question lay hidden in the shadows, waiting to be discovered – a shadow that stretched long and dark across the treacherous landscape of their mission. And the hunt was on.

CHAPTER 6

A Race Against Time

"In the wake of treachery, trust becomes a rare commodity. As shadows deepen and stakes rise, Cassie and Benjamin must navigate a maze of deceit to thwart a looming catastrophe."

The chilling revelation of the betrayal hung heavy in the air, a suffocating blanket of mistrust settling over Cassie and Benjamin. The comfortable familiarity forged in the crucible of the hostage crisis had shattered, replaced by a gnawing uncertainty about who to trust. The traitor's identity remained a phantom, a lurking danger in their midst, but the urgency of the situation demanded immediate action. Intelligence gleaned from the surviving hostage-taker suggested the conspitors' next move was imminent – a coordinated attack targeting multiple high-value assets across Europe, an attack designed to cripple global financial markets and plunge the world into chaos.

The clock was ticking. Benjamin, fueled by a potent blend of adrenaline and righteous anger, paced the dimly lit room. His usually meticulous mind felt scattered, the pieces of the puzzle refusing to coalesce into a coherent picture. Cassie, however, remained composed, her eyes sharp and focused. The betrayal, while a setback, hadn't broken her. Instead, it seemed to ignite a cold fury within her, sharpening her already keen instincts.

"We need to move fast," Cassie stated, her voice low and controlled. "Their next target is likely a financial institution in Zurich. We need to get there, disrupt their plan, and ideally, catch them in the act." Benjamin nodded, his gaze fixed on a grainy satellite image displayed on a monitor, showing the targeted bank. "Zurich That's a long shot. We need more intel." "We're working with what we have," Cassie retorted, already pulling up flight schedules on her laptop. "My contact in Interpol, Agent Dubois, has managed to pull some strings. We have a private jet standing by. We leave in two hours."

Their journey to Zurich was fraught with tension. The air crackled with unspoken questions, the weight of responsibility pressing down on them. Benjamin couldn't shake the feeling that they were walking into a trap, that the conspirators were expecting them. He glanced at Cassie, her face impassive, betraying nothing of her inner thoughts. He wondered what she was thinking, what secrets she was hiding. Their uneasy alliance was strained, tested by the betrayal and the looming threat.

Upon landing in Zurich, they were met by Agent Dubois, a seasoned Interpol operative with a cynical wit and a sharp eye for detail. He briefed them on their current intelligence, confirming their suspicions about the impending attack. The conspirators planned to use a sophisticated virus to cripple the bank's security systems, allowing them to remotely transfer billions of dollars into offshore accounts. The scale of the operation was staggering.

"We need to get inside that bank," Benjamin declared, his voice tight with urgency. "Before they activate the virus." Dubois shook his head. "It's a fortress, Moore. Impenetrable security. We'll need a way in, something... unconventional."

Cassie, her mind already racing, suggested a daring plan.
She had identified a potential weak point in thebank's security system: an obsolete ventilation shaft that ran directly into the server room. It was a risky maneuver, but it was their only chance. Under the cloak of darkness, they infiltrated the bank, moving silently through the labyrinthine corridors.

The tension was palpable, the silence broken only by the rhythmic thump of their hearts. Benjamin, using his detective skills, navigated the complex maze of security systems, while Cassie, with her expert knowledge of
negotiation tactics, expertly maneuvered them through any encounters with security guards, employing a mix of
persuasion and misdirection that was both breathtaking and terrifying. Every creak, every shadow, seemed to amplify the suspense.

Reaching the ventilation shaft, they faced a new challenge. The shaft was narrow and claustrophobic, its interior coated with a thick layer of dust and grime. They crawled through the suffocating darkness, the air thick with the metallic tang of rust and the faint scent of mildew. The journey was arduous, testing their physical and mental endurance.

The server room was their ultimate destination. Here, they faced their most formidable obstacle – the virus itself. A complex piece of malware designed to bypass even the most advanced security measures. Benjamin, with his technological expertise, worked to counteract the virus, a race against time against a sophisticated enemy. Cassie provided cover, her sharp awareness allowing them to avoid detection by the security cameras.

Just as the virus was about to execute its destructive payload, Benjamin managed to disable it. But their work was far from over. They still had to catch the conspirators. Using their combined skills and resources, they tracked the conspirators to a hidden underground facility, a clandestine lair where the true extent of their conspiracy unfolded. Inside the facility, they discovered a vast network of computers, servers, and data storage, revealing the true scope of the conspirators' ambitions. They were not merely seeking financial gain; they were planning to manipulate global markets, triggering a worldwide economic crisis that would allow them to seize control of key resources and establish a new world order. Their ambitions were terrifying, their reach extensive, and their network, deeply entrenched.

The final confrontation was a brutal battle of wits and strength. The conspirators were well-armed and prepared, but Cassie and Benjamin fought with the determination fueled by their shared goal and the threat to global security. They used their combined skills, deploying a mix of hand-to-hand combat, tactical maneuvers, and psychological warfare, pushing each other to their limits. After an intense physical confrontation, the perpetrators were subdued, but at a considerable personal cost. One of their allies, Agent Dubois, had been gravely injured in the process. He sustained life-threatening wounds during the fight.

The victory was bittersweet, achieved at a high price. As the authorities arrived to apprehend the perpetrators, they were left contemplating the devastating consequences of the conspiracy they had managed to thwart, the emotional toll, and the precarious alliance they had forged while facing a near-impossible task. Their work was far from over. The shadows of deception still lingered, casting long shadows over their future. The race against time had been won, but the war was far from over.

CHAPTER 7

Exploring the Conspirators Motives

"In the sterile quiet of the hospital, Cassie and Benjamin confronted the heavy weight of their discovery. The shadowy conspiracy they unearthed demanded not just courage but an unwavering resolve to dismantle an intricate web of deceit and power."

The sterile air of the hospital room hung heavy with antiseptic and unspoken anxieties. Agent Dubois, his face pale and drawn, lay in a medically induced coma, a silent testament to the brutality of their recent encounter. Cassie, her usual sharp demeanor softened by worry, sat by his bedside, her fingers tracing the faint lines of his scar tissue. Benjamin, his jaw tight with grim determination, paced restlessly, his mind already racing ahead, dissecting the fragmented clues they'd salvaged from the chaotic aftermath of the London operation.

The immediate threat had been neutralized, but the chilling reality remained: they had only scratched the surface of a vast and deeply entrenched conspiracy. The perpetrators apprehended were mere pawns, expendable pieces in a larger game orchestrated by shadowy figures operating from the furthest reaches of the globe. Their primary focus now shifted to understanding the conspirators' motives – the driving force behind this audacious plan to destabilize global financial markets.

Benjamin pulled out a thick file, its contents representing weeks of relentless investigation. "We have partial profiles on the apprehended operatives," he began, his voice low and measured. "Most were mercenaries, readily available for hire. They exhibited a high degree of professional training, indicating meticulous planning and significant financial backing." He tapped a photograph featuring a gaunt, almost skeletal man with piercing blue eyes. "This is Konstantin Volkov. He seemed to be the field commander, though his allegiances remain unclear."

Cassie leaned forward, her gaze intense. "Unclear? He directed the operation with chilling efficiency. There was no hesitation, no room for error. That suggests a level of
experience and loyalty that goes beyond a simple mercenary contract." She pointed to another photograph, this one showcasing a sophisticated woman with an unnerving calm in her eyes. "And this one, Irina Petrova. Her background is murky, but our preliminary analysis suggests ties to various international arms dealers."

The investigation led them down a rabbit hole of shell corporations, offshore accounts, and encrypted communications. Each unravelled thread revealed a new layer of complexity, a deeper network of individuals linked by a shared, albeit hidden, objective. The sheer scale of the operation was staggering. They were dealing with an organization capable of manipulating global financial
institutions, infiltrating high-security facilities, and recruiting individuals from all walks of life—all with seemingly little risk of exposure. The implications were terrifying. This wasn't just about money; it was about power, influence, and the potential for widespread chaos.

Their investigations uncovered a pattern: the conspirators targeted institutions with significant holdings in renewable energy technologies. This was no random act of terrorism; it was precisely calculated to disrupt the emerging clean energy sector. A theory began to solidify: this conspiracy was not solely driven by financial gain. The conspirators' motivations seemed to involve a deliberate attempt to hinder the global transition towards sustainable energy.

Further probing revealed a connection to a shadowy organization known only as "The Obsidian Circle." Their operational methodology pointed towards an organization with deep roots in the fossil fuel industry. The Obsidian Circle appeared to be comprised of powerful players who stood to lose the most from a shift towards renewable energy– energy moguls, heads of multinational corporations, and influential politicians who had a vested interest in maintaining the status quo.

Their vast wealth and influence gave them the means to orchestrate such an intricate and far-reaching scheme. They were playing a high-stakes game of global sabotage, betting on the failure of the green revolution to maintain their grip on power and wealth. Cassie and Benjamin delved into the history of The Obsidian Circle, piecing together fragments of information gleaned from leaked documents, intercepted communications, and confidential sources within intelligence agencies. Their investigation revealed a long history of clandestine operations funding political campaigns, influencing policy decisions, and even using underhanded tactics to eliminate competition. The Circle's influence extended far beyond the financial realm; they manipulated global markets, controlled information flows, and even had fingers in the intelligence agencies themselves.

Their network was a spider's web, its threads woven through multiple continents, intricately layered to ensure anonymity and operational security. They were masters of deception, masters of disguise, employing intricate layers of encryption and using proxies to distance themselves from their actions. Their modus operandi was precise and cold-blooded. They didn't engage in overt displays of power; instead, they operated in the shadows, manipulating events from a distance, orchestrating chaos from behind a veil of secrecy.

The more they uncovered, the more they realized the scope of their task. They were not just facing criminals; they were battling a well-organized, highly sophisticated organization with a deeply entrenched history and practically unlimited resources. The implications extended far beyond financial markets; the potential for global instability, political upheaval, and widespread social unrest were alarming. This was a battle for the future itself, a fight to prevent a deliberate unraveling of the global order. One intriguing piece of intelligence emerged: a possible connection between The Obsidian Circle and a retired high-ranking military officer, General Petrov, known for his hardline views and close ties to several prominent energy companies.

General Petrov, despite his retirement, still commanded significant influence within the military and political establishments. His reputation for ruthlessness and his network of loyalists further complicated their efforts. Was General Petrov the mastermind behind the organization, or simply a highly placed collaborator? The investigation took them to several locations: from the opulent villas of Monaco to the secluded mountain hideouts in Switzerland. Each location revealed more clues, more layers of deceit, and more dangerous individuals involved in this conspiracy. The hunt became a relentless chase, a cat-and-mouse game of wits and intelligence, a battle against time to expose the truth before the Obsidian Circle could execute the next phase of their plan.

The trail led them across borders, into clandestine meetings, and to the heart of a conspiracy that threatened to redefine the world order. As the investigation progressed, Cassie and Benjamin's uneasy alliance deepened, forged in the fires of their shared pursuit of justice. Their initial mistrust slowly gave way to a grudging respect, their differing approaches complementing each other. Benjamin's methodical approach to investigation was perfectly balanced by Cassie's sharp instincts and ability to read people's intentions. They became an effective team, capable of navigating the treacherous waters of international espionage and the complexities of global politics. They knew that failure was not an option. The fate of the world, or so it seemed, rested on their shoulders.

The weight of responsibility bore heavily on them, the constant threat of betrayal and the ever-present danger a constant companion. Their task was not just to apprehend the perpetrators but to dismantle the entire organization, to expose the Obsidian Circle and bring its leaders to justice.

The journey would be long and fraught with peril, requiring more than just skill and bravery; it demanded unwavering determination, steadfast loyalty, and an unyielding pursuit of truth. The shadows of deception still loomed large, threatening to engulf them at any moment. But Cassie and Benjamin were ready. Their fight for justice had just begun.

CHAPTER 8

Unexpected Ally

"In the shadows of deception, alliances are forged on fragile trust. As Cassie and Benjamin navigate the treacherous path of hidden agendas, the line between friend and foe blurs, and the stakes grow ever higher."

The rhythmic beeping of Dubois's life support machine provided a stark counterpoint to the low hum of the city outside. Cassie, exhausted but resolute, hadn't left his side since the operation. Benjamin, meanwhile, was immersed in a world of encrypted emails and hastily scribbled notes, the faint scent of stale coffee clinging to his clothes. The Obsidian Circle remained a shadowy enigma, their motives as elusive as their members. They knew the organization was vast, its tentacles reaching into the highest echelons of power, but concrete evidence remained maddeningly scarce.

A sudden vibration from Benjamin's burner phone broke the tense silence. He glanced at the screen, a flicker of surprise crossing his face. It was an anonymous encrypted message, a single line: *"Meet me. The Serpent's Tooth. Midnight."*

The Serpent's Tooth. A notorious, abandoned speakeasy tucked away in the labyrinthine alleys of London's East End, a place whispered about in hushed tones, a haven for informants, double agents, and those operating in the
shadows. The very idea sent a chill down Cassie's spine. It was a place where one wrong move could be fatal. "What is it?" Cassie asked, her voice low.

Benjamin hesitated, his gaze fixed on the message. "It's a location. The Serpent's Tooth. An anonymous tip. We have no idea who it is." Cassie's intuition screamed caution. "It could be a trap. A set-up." "It could be," Benjamin conceded, "but the message… it's specific. Too specific to ignore. Besides, we're running out of leads." He looked at her, his eyes filled with a weariness that belied his usual sharp demeanor. "We need to take a chance."

The decision was made, the risk reluctantly accepted. At midnight, shrouded in the cloak of darkness, Cassie and Benjamin found themselves navigating the claustrophobic alleyways, the air thick with the stench of decay and damp earth. The Serpent's Tooth was a dilapidated building, its once-grand facade crumbling under the weight of neglect and time. Inside, the air was thick with cigarette smoke, the low murmur of hushed conversations a constant background noise.

They found their contact seated alone in a dimly lit corner booth, a figure cloaked in shadow, their face obscured by the low light and a wide-brimmed hat. As they approached, the figure slowly removed the hat, revealing a woman with striking, emerald green eyes and a cascade of fiery red hair.

Her name, she introduced herself, was Anya Petrova, a former intelligence operative with a reputation as a ghost. "I have information about the Obsidian Circle," Anya said, her voice low and husky, tinged with a slight Russian accent. "Information that could bring them down." Over the next few hours, Anya revealed a network of offshore accounts, hidden communication channels, and the identities of several key players within the Obsidian Circle.

The information was staggering, its implications far-reaching and deeply disturbing. It painted a picture of a vast conspiracy, a carefully constructed web of deceit and corruption that extended into the highest levels of government and international finance. But as Anya spoke, a growing unease settled over Cassie and Benjamin. Her information was incredibly valuable, almost too valuable. It was too perfectly timed, too precisely detailed. It felt almost…orchestrated. "Why are you helping us?" Benjamin asked, his voice sharp. He didn't trust easily, especially not someone with Anya's shadowy past.

Anya smiled, a chillingly captivating smile that revealed just a hint of something unsettling behind her emerald eyes."Let's just say I have my own reasons for wanting the
Obsidian Circle destroyed," she replied, her gaze unwavering. "And your methods…they are…efficient."

The ambiguity of her words hung heavy in the air. What were her true motives? Was she a genuine ally or a double agent, playing a dangerous game of her own? The question gnawed at Benjamin, fueling his inherent skepticism. Cassie, however, felt a flicker of something else - a sense of cautious optimism. Anya's information was too accurate, too specific to be fabricated. But trusting her was a gamble, a dangerous game of trust with incredibly high stakes.

The meeting ended as abruptly as it began. Anya vanished into the shadows as quickly as she'd appeared, leaving Cassie and Benjamin to grapple with the implications of her revelations. The information she provided was a significant breakthrough, providing them with a roadmap to dismantle the Obsidian Circle, but the uncertainty surrounding her allegiance remained a constant, nagging worry.

The journey to expose the Obsidian Circle was far from over. Anya's help was a lifeline, but it was a lifeline tethered to a question mark. Her cryptic motivations, her mysterious past, and her sudden appearance left them with more questions than answers. They had to proceed cautiously, verifying her information while simultaneously considering the possibility of a double-cross. The shadows of deception remained, but they were now illuminated by a single, flickering candle—the uncertain light of an unexpected ally.

The following days were a blur of frantic activity. Cassie, using her unique negotiating skills, established contact with several key informants from Anya's intel, carefully extracting information and verifying its authenticity. Benjamin, meanwhile, worked relentlessly with the police department, meticulously piecing together the puzzle provided by Anya, using her information to identify and locate key players in the Obsidian Circle. Every piece of verified information was a victory, pushing them closer to their objective.

They discovered a pattern, a disturbingly meticulous methodology behind the Obsidian Circle's operations. It wasn't about simple financial gain; it was about something far more sinister - a carefully orchestrated plan to destabilize several key global economies through targeted financial manipulations and politically motivated assassinations. The scale of their ambitions was breathtaking in its audacity, the potential consequences almost too horrifying to contemplate.

As they delved deeper, they unearthed links between the Obsidian Circle and several high-ranking government officials, confirming their suspicions about the organization's far-reaching influence. Each revelation heightened the stakes, amplifying the sense of urgency. They were facing a sophisticated adversary, an adversary with resources and connections far beyond their initial estimations. The fight had become a battle against time, a race against the Obsidian Circle's well-laid plans.

In the midst of the relentless investigation, the uncertainty surrounding Anya remained a constant undercurrent. They had cautiously tested her information, verifying multiple points of contact, confirming several of her disclosures. Yet, the nagging question persisted: was Anya genuinely assisting them, or was she manipulating them, using them to achieve her own, unknown goals? Her cryptic comments, her enigmatic smile, the sheer audacity of her offer – it all pointed towards a hidden agenda.

The next move needed to be calculated, a delicate balancing act between using Anya's intel and safeguarding themselves from her potential betrayal. The weight of the situation pressed heavily on them, the fragile alliance a precarious bridge built on a foundation of uncertainty. They needed a plan, a strategy that acknowledged the potential for treachery and simultaneously capitalized on Anya's invaluable contributions.

The shadows of deception still loomed, but with each confirmed piece of information, a sense of cautious optimism began to take root. Their pursuit of justice was far from over, but they were moving closer to exposing the truth behind the Obsidian Circle, inching their way
towards unveiling its insidious machinations and bringing down its architects. The next chapter, however, promised to be fraught with even greater danger and uncertainty. The game was far from over.

CHAPTER 9

Navigating Treacherous Territory

"In the dim alleys of Paris, shadows whispered secrets of power and betrayal. As Cassie and Benjamin closed in on the Obsidian Circle, the line between ally and enemy blurred, thrusting them into a deadly game of survival."

The Parisian alley reeked of stale cigarettes and desperation. Rain slicked the cobblestones, reflecting the neon glow of a nearby bar in shimmering puddles. Cassie, her trench coat pulled tight against the chill, felt a prickle of unease. This wasn't the sterile environment of a London hospital; this was the underbelly of Paris, a place where shadows held secrets and whispers carried the weight of centuries. Benjamin, his usual sharp demeanor softened by fatigue, followed close behind, his hand resting on the butt of his holstered weapon. Anya, their volatile informant, led the way, her movements fluid and silent, a phantom in the city's nocturnal labyrinth.

Anya stopped abruptly, her hand brushing against a damp brick wall. "Here," she breathed, her voice barely audible above the city's murmur. "This is where they meet."

The building was nondescript, a crumbling apartment block swallowed by the night. No identifying markers, no flashy signage – just another piece of the Parisian puzzle. Cassie scanned the surroundings, her trained eyes searching for anything out of place, any sign of surveillance. Nothing. The Obsidian Circle was meticulous, their operations shrouded in a veil of secrecy. This meeting, however, was crucial.

Anya had assured them that high-ranking members would be present, individuals with direct knowledge of the organization's global network. Benjamin, ever the pragmatist, was already devising a plan. "We need to establish surveillance," he murmured, pulling out a small, sophisticated listening device. "But we can't risk a direct approach. They're too well-connected." Cassie nodded, her mind already racing. A direct confrontation would be suicide. Their best option was to observe, to gather intelligence without revealing their presence. They needed to know the structure of the Obsidian Circle, their operational methods, and, most importantly, their ultimate goal. The stakes were too high to risk a premature move.

They spent the next few hours establishing a perimeter, using their combined expertise to navigate the treacherous streets and find optimal vantage points. Benjamin's knowledge of surveillance techniques complemented Cassie's ability to blend seamlessly into any environment. Anya, despite her unpredictable nature, proved to be a surprisingly valuable asset, her familiarity with the local underworld giving them access to otherwise impenetrable areas.

As the meeting time approached, a nervous energy filled the air. The rain had stopped, and the city seemed to hold its breath, anticipating the arrival of the Obsidian Circle's elite. A black sedan, nondescript and unmarked, pulled up to the building. Two men emerged, their faces partially obscured by shadows, their movements betraying a practiced air of nonchalance. They were followed by a third, a woman, her elegance a stark contrast to the gritty urban setting. The group vanished inside, leaving the trio to observe.

Using their advanced listening equipment, they intercepted fragments of the conversation, snippets of coded language and cryptic discussions that only served to deepen the mystery. They learned of a vast network of operatives spread across the globe, of intricate financial schemes that laundered billions, and of a hidden agenda that threatened to destabilize entire nations. The Obsidian Circle wasn't just a criminal organization; it was a sophisticated, highly organized conspiracy with global reach.

As the hours passed, the magnitude of the threat became increasingly clear. The Obsidian Circle wasn't just after money or power; they were after something far more sinister– something that could trigger a global catastrophe. The realization hit them with the force of a physical blow. Their mission had escalated from a simple hostage rescue to a battle to prevent a world-altering event.

The meeting concluded with a flurry of hushed whispers and furtive glances. The group departed as swiftly as they had arrived, melting into the night like shadows. Anya, her face pale with apprehension, turned to Cassie and Benjamin. "They know," she said, her voice trembling slightly. "They know someone's watching."

Cassie felt a chill run down her spine. Their cover was blown. They had gathered invaluable intelligence, but at a considerable cost. Now, they had to escape, to disappear without a trace, before the Obsidian Circle could unleash their wrath. The Parisian alley, once a mere backdrop to their operation, had become a battleground, a deadly game of cat and mouse where the stakes were nothing less than their lives.

Their escape was a desperate race against time, a heart-pounding pursuit through the labyrinthine streets of Paris. The Obsidian Circle's operatives, swift and relentless, were close behind. Every alleyway was a potential ambush, every shadow held the threat of capture. Cassie, using her extensive knowledge of street fighting, skillfully navigated the urban maze, fighting off pursuers with lethal efficiency. Benjamin, his tactical skills honed from years of police work, used his superior intelligence to anticipate their opponents' moves, orchestrating their escape with precision and finesse. Anya, her familiarity with the hidden pathways and back alleys of the city, was a vital guide, steering them away from potential traps and dead ends.

They finally found refuge in a secluded courtyard, their breath coming in ragged gasps, their bodies trembling with exhaustion and adrenaline. The sound of pursuing footsteps faded into the distance, leaving them in the uneasy silence of victory. They had escaped, but the ordeal had taken its toll. The close call served as a stark reminder of the perilous nature of their mission and the immense power of the organization they were facing. The weight of their responsibility, the gravity of the situation, pressed heavily upon their shoulders.

The escape had been a success, but it had also exposed the deep-seated flaws in their plan. Their reliance on Anya's intelligence, while valuable, had proven to be a double-edged sword. Her unpredictable nature and close ties to the Obsidian Circle had exposed their operation, leaving them vulnerable. They had won a battle, but the war was far from over.

The next steps needed careful consideration. They couldn't continue to rely on Anya's information; they needed a more reliable, internal source. Their initial strategy of observation had yielded vital intelligence, but it had been achieved at the cost of their anonymity. They needed to rethink their approach and formulate a more comprehensive plan that accounted for the evolving threat.As they sat in the hushed quiet of the courtyard, the weight of their task pressed down upon them. The Parisian night, once a backdrop to their operation, had become a witness to their struggle. The escape had been a harrowing experience, but it had bought them time – precious time to regroup, refine their strategy and prepare for the next stage of their deadly game.

The shadows of deception still loomed, but now they were armed with invaluable knowledge, and a renewed determination to bring down the Obsidian Circle, whatever the cost. The journey was far from over, but they were prepared to face whatever challenges lay ahead. The stakes were higher than ever before; the fate of the world hung in the balance.

CHAPTER 10

A Close Call

"In the labyrinthine streets of Paris, betrayal lurked in every shadow. As Cassie and Benjamin raced against time, the line between ally and enemy blurred, thrusting them into a deadly game where survival was the only rule."

The Renault, a battered but reliable vehicle Anya had somehow procured, screeched around a corner, its tires spitting gravel. Inside, Cassie gripped the worn leather seat, her knuckles white. Benjamin, his eyes scanning the rearview mirror, muttered a silent prayer. Anya, ever the picture of controlled chaos, navigated the Parisian backstreets with unnerving precision, her gaze fixed on the winding road ahead. The escape had been a frantic scramble, a chaotic ballet of gunfire and adrenaline. They'd been cornered, ambushed in a narrow alleyway, the kind that swallowed sound and light, leaving only the chilling echo of gunshots.

Three figures, their faces obscured by shadows and balaclavas, had emerged from the darkness, their weapons trained on them. The initial volley had been devastating; a hail of bullets that ripped through the air, narrowly missing them. Benjamin, ever the pragmatist, had reacted instantly, pushing Cassie to the ground, their bodies shielded by the sturdy stone wall of a centuries-old building. The ensuing firefight had been brutal, a chaotic dance of death played out under the flickering gaslight. Anya, surprisingly agile despite her slight frame, had provided cover, her own weapon spitting fire with deadly accuracy. She was a phantom, a whirlwind of motion, disappearing and reappearing, her movements blurring in the dim light.

Cassie, despite her years of experience negotiating with terrorists and hardened criminals, had felt a cold knot of fear tighten in her stomach. This wasn't a calculated risk, a strategic maneuver; this was a blind, desperate struggle for survival. The sheer brutality of the attack, the cold precision of their assailants, had shaken her. They weren't just ordinary thugs; these were professionals, highly trained, deadly efficient. The chilling realization washed over her – they were hunting them.

The escape had been a near miss, a matter of inches, of seconds. A stray bullet had grazed Benjamin's arm, a minor wound that bled freely, staining his dark shirt crimson. Anya had suffered a superficial graze to her leg, a testament to her agility and skill. But Cassie, miraculously, had emerged unscathed, a fact that she attributed to nothing short of pure luck. The adrenaline still coursed through her veins, a potent cocktail of fear and exhilaration.

As they sped away, leaving the scene of the ambush behind, a chilling silence descended upon the car. The nearness of death hung heavy in the air, a tangible presence that threatened to suffocate them. Benjamin, despite his injury, remained stoic, his gaze fixed on the road ahead. He was a man of action, of practicality, and he refused to let fear paralyze him. But Cassie could sense the tension coiled within him, the barely suppressed furythat simmered beneath his calm exterior. Anya, her breathing ragged, broke the silence. "They knew we were coming," she whispered, her voice barely audible above the engine's roar. "Someone betrayed us."

The accusation hung in the air, unspoken, yet heavy with implication. The betrayal stung, a bitter pill to swallow. Their entire operation rested on trust, on a delicate web of alliances and secrets. Now, that trust had been shattered, the web unraveling, threatening to bring them all down. "Who?" Benjamin asked, his voice low and dangerous. His hand instinctively went to his injured arm, wincing slightly at the sharp pain that shot through him. The question was sharp, pointed, demanding an answer.

Anya hesitated, her eyes darting between Benjamin and Cassie. "I don't know for sure," she admitted, her voice strained. "But there are only a few people who knew about this... and they all have their reasons to betray us." The silence returned, thick and suffocating. The city lights whizzed past, blurring into streaks of color. The weight of their predicament pressed down on them, a crushing burden of uncertainty and danger. They were playing a deadly game, a game where the stakes were life and death, and where betrayal lurked around every corner.

They finally reached a safe house, a dilapidated apartment building tucked away in a quiet corner of the city. The air inside was stale and damp, but it offered a temporary respite from the relentless pursuit. Benjamin, despite his injury, insisted on examining the weapon that had been used in the ambush. He carefully examined the markings, his keen eyes picking out minute details that would help them identify the weapon's origin and the group responsible for the attack. Cassie watched him, a mixture of admiration and concern etched on her face. She knew that Benjamin was a brilliant detective, a man who could extract information from the smallest clues.

The weapon was sophisticated, military-grade, not something easily acquired on the black market. This confirmed their suspicions; they weren't dealing with a small-time gang; they were up against a highly organized and well-funded criminal organization. The implications were chilling. This organization possessed the resources and the manpower to carry out large-scale operations, operations that could potentially destabilize entire countries. "This is bigger than we thought," Cassie said, breaking the silence. She studied Benjamin's face, seeing the same realization reflected in his eyes.

The initial operation, the rescue mission in London, had seemed significant, a matter of life and death. But now, they were realizing that this was merely a small piece of a much larger puzzle, a puzzle that spanned continents and involved powerful players. "We need to contact Dimitri," Benjamin said, his voice tight with grim determination. Dimitri, his twin brother, was a Navy SEAL, and his expertise in military operations was invaluable. Their sibling bond was complicated, but in this moment, it was a crucial link in their desperate struggle for survival. They had to take their collaboration to a new level.

Anya nodded, her eyes filled with a mixture of apprehension and resolve. "He's the only one who can help us now." They needed more than just their skills, their experience, and their cunning. They needed the power and resources of a highly effective military organization. They needed to call in all the backup they could possibly find, and quickly.

The phone call to Dimitri was tense. He listened to their account of the ambush, his voice a calm counterpoint to their frantic narrative. He understood the gravity of the situation, the danger they were in. He agreed to meet them, to help them unravel the conspiracy that had ensnared them. But his words also carried a note of caution, a warning that the danger was far greater than they had initially imagined. The meeting with Dimitri was held in a secure location, a heavily fortified compound on the outskirts of Paris. The atmosphere was charged with tension, the air thick with unspoken apprehension. Dimitri, a man of few words but unwavering resolve, listened intently to their account of the events, his gaze sharp and piercing. He had a way of assessing a situation, cutting through the noise and getting to the heart of the matter. He had the innate ability to detect when someone was lying, regardless of how well they prepared for the confrontation.

He provided them with access to advanced technology, intelligence gathered from various sources, and an array of resources that would enable them to confront their enemy. He laid out a new strategy, a plan that was both bold and audacious. Their fight for survival would require intelligence, precision, and a calculated risk. They were up against a sophisticated organization and they needed to be equally organized and prepared. It wouldn't just be about outsmarting them, it would also be about outfighting them. As the meeting concluded, a sense of grim determination settled over them. The shadows of deception still loomed, but they were no longer alone. They had each other, and they had Dimitri.

The fight would be long and dangerous, but they were ready. The stakes were higher than ever; the fate of the world might depend on their success. The next phase of their mission would require unparalleled skill and absolute trust. And the clock was ticking. The pursuit continued; the game was far from over. They needed to find out who betrayed them. They needed to find out who was pulling the strings. And most importantly, they needed to stop them. The world depended on it.

CHAPTER 11

Identifying the Traitor

"In the dim glow of the interrogation room, the weight of betrayal hung heavy. As Cassie and Benjamin faced the traitor in their midst, the line between friend and foe blurred, setting the stage for a battle that was as personal as it was dangerous."

The air in the small, dimly lit interrogation room hung thick with the scent of stale coffee and unspoken accusations. Cassie, her usually impeccable composure slightly frayed, leaned forward, her gaze fixed on the man across the table. He was a senior MI6 agent, a man she had once considered an ally, a man named Alistair Finch. The betrayal stung, a sharp, bitter taste in her mouth. It was Finch's seemingly innocuous information leak that had almost cost them everything in the London hostage crisis. Now, the stakes were even higher. The global conspiracy they'd stumbled upon was far bigger, far more dangerous than they had ever imagined, and Finch was at its heart.

Benjamin, his jaw tight with suppressed anger, watched Finch from the shadows. The betrayal cut deeper for him. He'd known Finch for years, respected him, even considered him a friend within the professional confines of their shared world. The thought of Finch's treachery twisting a knife into the already fragile trust between himself and Cassie gnawed at him. This wasn't just a case; this was personal. He'd have to put aside his grief for justice.

Their investigation had led them down a rabbit hole of
encrypted communications, shadowy meetings in dimly lit pubs, and coded messages hidden within seemingly innocuous documents. Each new discovery peeled back a layer of the conspiracy, revealing a network of double agents, moles, and compromised officials stretching across continents. They'd painstakingly reconstructed the traitor's movements, piecing together fragments of information like a shattered mirror. The trail was intricate, deliberately obfuscated, designed to mislead and confuse.

The initial suspect had been obvious – the seemingly expendable contact who'd passed them faulty intelligence.
But Cassie, ever the pragmatist, refused to accept simple explanations. The leak had been too precise, too damaging. It wasn't a simple error; it was a calculated betrayal. Finch had been present during the critical stages of the negotiation in London, seemingly acting as a liaison between the police and MI6, providing tactical insights that should have helped Cassie. Instead, his so-called insights had subtly guided the hostage-takers, leading them into a deadly trap.

His apparent carelessness had been the catalyst of a chain reaction, almost resulting in the death of innocent people. "We have evidence," Cassie stated, her voice low and controlled, "placing you at several locations crucial to the conspirators' operations. Locations you shouldn't have known about. Locations only accessible to someone deeply embedded within their network." She laid a file on the table, the weight of its contents palpable.

Finch remained impassive, his eyes betraying nothing. He was a master of deception, a chameleon who could blend into any environment. He was also a master manipulator, adept at using charm and intimidation to achieve his goals. "Evidence? You have circumstantial evidence, Agent Davies. It proves nothing." His voice was smooth, devoid of emotion. It was a voice he'd honed over years of manipulating information and people.

Benjamin stepped forward, his gaze piercing. "The encryption on the messages you passed to them was identical to the one used by the organization's leader. It's not a coincidence, Finch. You're part of it." He let his words hang in the air, the unspoken threat as sharp as a blade.

The ensuing interrogation was a tense dance between deception and truth. Finch denied everything, his responses carefully calculated, measured. But the subtle shifts in his body language, the fleeting hesitations, betrayed his carefully constructed facade.

Cassie and Benjamin meticulously deconstructed his claims, revealing inconsistencies and contradictions, using his own meticulously constructed alibis against him. They even discovered coded messages hidden in his seemingly harmless emails and even within the metadata of photographs of his family. The details seemed so small, so trivial on their own, but when combined, formed a damning case.

Hours bled into one another, the tension in the room growing with every passing moment. Cassie and Benjamin worked in tandem, their contrasting styles surprisingly complementary. Cassie, with her sharp analytical mind and honed negotiation skills, expertly exploited Finch's weaknesses, picking apart his lies with surgical precision. Benjamin, with his years of experience in criminal investigations, focused on the details, meticulously building a concrete case from circumstantial evidence.

The turning point came not during a direct confrontation, but through a seemingly minor detail – an old photograph on Finch's desk. It was a casual snapshot of him with a woman, her face partially obscured, taken at a high-profile diplomatic function in Geneva. Benjamin had originally dismissed it as meaningless, but Cassie's sharp eye noticed something amiss– a faint, almost imperceptible symbol embroidered on the woman's dress. The same symbol that had appeared in several coded messages they had intercepted. The woman, they discovered, was a known associate of the conspiracy's leader.

The photograph placed Finch directly into the network, providing the irrefutable evidence they needed. The revelation shook Finch. For the first time, his composure wavered, a flicker of fear crossing his eyes. The carefully constructed mask of professionalism crumbled, revealing the cold, calculating man underneath. He broke down under the relentless pressure, finally confessing to his involvement in the conspiracy. He spilled the details—the elaborate plan to destabilize global markets, the methods used to manipulate governments and individuals, and the identities of other key players in the organization.

His confession was a cascade of information, a flood of details about the conspiracy. He revealed his motivations—not greed, but a twisted sense of loyalty to a cause he believed in, fueled by a deep-seated resentment towards the international power structures he was once a part of. His confession painted a bleak picture—a world manipulated by forces operating in the shadows, pulling strings from behind closed doors. With Finch's confession, the picture sharpened considerably.

They now had a concrete lead, a foothold into the heart of the conspiracy. But his confession also revealed a deeper level of treachery. Finch's confession revealed a hidden layer to the organization. A seemingly benevolent charity, masking illicit activities designed to exploit and manipulate on a global scale. The interrogation ended, but the struggle was far from over. Finch's information was crucial, but it also brought a new set of challenges. The consequences of his betrayal were far-reaching, shaking the foundations of their alliances and threatening to unravel everything they had worked for. The weight of their discovery hung heavy in the air, a chilling reminder of the vast and dangerosusworld they were now navigating.

Their hunt for the conspirators continued, but the lines between allies and enemies were now thoroughly blurred, the trust once held so dear, now broken and scattered like shards of glass. The quest for justice continued, but they now knew, with a certainty that chilled them to the bone, that the fight was far from over.

CHAPTER 12

Uncovering Hidden Agendas

The chill of the London night seeped into Cassie's bones, a stark contrast to the simmering fury inside her. Finch's confession, while revealing, had left more questions than answers. The conspiracy ran deeper than a simple information leak; it was a meticulously crafted web of deceit, woven by players whose motives remained shrouded in mystery. Benjamin, his usually sharp features etched with a grim determination, stood beside her, the weight of their discovery pressing down on them both.

Their investigation led them to a clandestine meeting in a secluded warehouse district. Intelligence suggested a rendezvous between a known arms dealer, a shadowy figure only identified as "Seraph," and a high-ranking official within the French Ministry of Defence. The operation was fraught with risk. The warehouse was heavily guarded, patrolled by men who moved with the practiced ease of seasoned mercenaries.

Their mission: surveillance, observation, gathering enough evidence to solidify their suspicions before making a move. Under the cover of darkness, they moved like ghosts, Benjamin's tactical expertise complementing Cassie's negotiation skills, skills that extended beyond the verbal. Their movements were fluid, a practiced dance of shadow and silence. They set up observation points, using high-powered binoculars and sophisticated listening devices, technology provided by a reluctant but ultimately helpful contact within the NSA. The warehouse, a concrete monolith, seemed to pulsate with unseen energy, the hum of clandestine activity a tangible presence in the night. The meeting unfolded slowly, a tense ballet of veiled threats and carefully chosen words. Seraph, a gaunt man with eyes that held the cold glint of steel, spoke in clipped, precise sentences, his words carrying the weight of untold power.

The French official, a man named Dubois, a decorated general, appeared nervous, his attempts at maintaining composure betraying his unease. Their conversation revealed fragments of a larger plan, a plot involving the destabilization of several key Middle Eastern countries, a scheme designed to create a vacuum of power that Seraph intended to fill, controlling the flow of arms and influence in the region. But there was more, a subtext running beneath their overt dialogue. Cassie, her keen observation skills honed over years of negotiation, picked up on subtle nuances – the almost imperceptible shift in Dubois's posture, the way Seraph's gaze lingered for a fraction too long on a seemingly innocuous object in the room. She sensed a hidden agenda, something beyond the arms deal and the political destabilization. She noticed a small, almost imperceptible symbol tattooed on Seraph's wrist, a symbol she recognized from her previous undercover work, a symbol associated with a long-dormant, ultra-nationalist group known as "The Obsidian Hand."

Benjamin, meanwhile, was focusing on the technical aspects. He had managed to tap into the warehouse's security system, providing them with a live feed of their movements and conversations. He discovered that the warehouse's seemingly impenetrable security system was being remotely monitored from a secondary location. This discovery added another layer of complexity to their already precarious situation. It suggested that even if they managed to extract evidence from the current encounter, someone else already had full access to their actions. The stakes had suddenly become much higher.

As the night wore on, the puzzle pieces began to fall into place. The double agent wasn't just Finch; it was a far larger network. The Obsidian Hand was not just a dormant group. It was a highly organized and well-funded organization, pulling strings within governments and military structures, their true goal still cloaked in secrecy. The arms deal, the political instability – these were merely tools, pieces in a larger, more sinister game. The revelation left them both reeling. The meeting concluded with an exchange of encrypted data, a silent transfer of power and control. Cassie and Benjamin, unseen and unheard, watched as Seraph and Dubois departed, leaving behind a trail of suspicion and unanswered questions. The evidence they'd gathered was compelling, but it was only a fraction of the truth. The extent of the conspiracy was vast, its tentacles reaching into the highest echelons of power.

The next few days were a blur of frantic activity. They worked tirelessly, analyzing the data they'd collected, piecing together the fragments of information into a coherent narrative. They identified patterns, connections they hadn't noticed before. Each new discovery led to another, a cascade of revelations that forced them to confront the sheer scale of the threat. Their investigation led them to a previously unknown subsidiary of a multinational corporation, a seemingly benign entity involved in humanitarian aid. However, their research revealed that this corporation was a front, a cleverly disguised conduit for funding the Obsidian Hand. The implications were staggering. The corporation's extensive network of global operations allowed the Obsidian Hand to move freely, undetected, infiltrating governments and military institutions with ease.

They discovered the existence of a hidden server farm, located deep within a decommissioned military base, containing encrypted communication logs between Seraph, Dubois, and other high-ranking officials from various countries. Accessing this server farm became their next priority. Gaining access to the farm was a major hurdle. It was guarded by state-of-the-art security systems and personnel highly trained in counter-intelligence. Benjamin's technical skills, combined with Cassie's knowledge of psychology and negotiation, were crucial in designing the infiltration strategy.

They decided to use a two-pronged approach. Benjamin would focus on hacking into the system remotely, exploiting vulnerabilities he identified in the security protocols. Simultaneously, Cassie would employ social engineering techniques to gain access to the physical location, using her persuasion skills to manipulate those guarding the site. The operation required precision, timing, and a degree of calculated risk. The plan unfolded meticulously, each step executed with precision and calculated risk. Benjamin's expertise bypassed the security protocols, while Cassie, employing her unique skills, used social engineering tactics to bypass the guards and gain physical access to the server facility. Their combined efforts allowed them to download the encrypted data.

The data revealed a shocking truth. The Obsidian Hand's ultimate goal was not just regional destabilization; it was global dominance. They planned to trigger a series of coordinated attacks on key global infrastructure, plunging the world into chaos and creating a vacuum of power they could exploit. The sheer audacity of their plan was breathtaking, a testament to their cunning and ambition. Armed with this information, Cassie and Benjamin knew they had to act swiftly. They presented their findings to their respective agencies, but the response was less than enthusiastic. Their findings were too explosive, too far-reaching to be readily accepted. Trust, already fractured, was further eroded by the enormity of their discovery. They were facing powerful forces, deeply entrenched within the system they had sworn to protect.

The path ahead was fraught with peril. They knew that they were not only fighting against a powerful enemy, but also against the skepticism and inertia of their own organizations. The realization that the conspiracy went so deep, that the trust that held the world together was a fragile façade, instilled a chilling sense of foreboding. Their journey was far from over.

The fight for justice, for global safety, was just beginning. The double agent was merely a pawn in a larger game, and uncovering the true architects of this global conspiracy would require every ounce of their skill, courage, and resilience. The weight of the world rested on their shoulders, and the stakes could not be higher.

CHAPTER 13

A Desperate Gamble

"As the wind howled through London's shadowed alleys, Cassie and Benjamin braced themselves for the next move in their high-stakes game. With each step closer to the heart of a global conspiracy, the shadows deepened and trust became a dangerous gamble. The tendrils of betrayal were tightening, and the true puppet masters were watching."

The biting London wind whipped around Cassie and Benjamin as they huddled in the shadowed alleyway, the city's nocturnal hum a dissonant soundtrack to their clandestine meeting. Finch's confession had painted a grim picture, a vast conspiracy stretching across continents, its tendrils wrapped around the highest echelons of power. Their initial shock had given way to a grim determination, a shared understanding that their fight was far from over. They had a double agent, yes, but who was pulling the strings? That was the question that gnawed at them both.

Benjamin, his jaw clenched tight, tapped a series of codes on his phone, his movements quick and precise. "I've managed to trace the encrypted communication Finch mentioned to a server based in Zurich," he whispered, his voice low and urgent. "It's heavily protected, military-grade encryption. We'll need a significant diversion to get in."

Cassie, ever the pragmatist, weighed the risks. A direct assault on a Swiss server farm, even with the resources of Interpol and the Metropolitan Police at their disposal, was a long shot. It would be a blatant act of aggression, potentially sparking an international incident. "We need something less... conspicuous," she said, her gaze fixed on the swirling fog that clung to the alleyway. "Something that will draw their attention elsewhere." A dangerous idea began to take shape in her mind, a plan that bordered on reckless, a desperate gamble. It was a high-stakes game of chess, where they were playing against an unseen opponent, one who held all the pieces. But if they didn't play boldly, if they didn't take chances, they stood no chance of winning.

The stakes were far too high to play it safe. "I have a contact," she finally said, her voice barely a whisper. "An old friend, let's call him 'Ghost'. He operates in the shadows, providing intelligence to various agencies, often bending the rules – or breaking them outright. He owes me a favour." Benjamin raised an eyebrow. "Ghost? This sounds... risky, Cassie." "It is," she admitted, her eyes betraying a flicker of apprehension. "But he's the only one who could pull this off. He has access to resources and networks that are beyond our reach. He can create the distraction we need – a carefully orchestrated chaos, designed to divert the attention of whoever controls the Zurich server."

They spent the next few hours meticulously outlining their plan. Ghost would create a fake cyberattack on a seemingly unrelated target – a major European bank – drawing the Swiss authorities and cybersecurity experts into a frenzy. While they were preoccupied, Benjamin, using a combination of hacking skills and inside contacts, would infiltrate the Zurich server, hoping to get to the data before their enemies realized what was happening.

Cassie, meanwhile, would act as a double agent, maintaining her existing contact with the known double agent, feeding the opposing side false information while simultaneously monitoring their communication for any telltale signs of their true intentions. It was a delicate dance on the razor's edge of deception, a risky maneuver requiring flawless execution.

The operation was set for three days later. The timing was crucial. They needed enough time to prepare and coordinate, while also creating a sense of urgency and unpredictability. The next few days were a blur of frantic activity. Benjamin worked tirelessly, refining the hacking protocols and creating backdoors in anticipation of potential countermeasures. Cassie, meanwhile, maintained her communication with Finch's handler, subtly manipulating them and collecting information. She had to build trust, earning their confidence without giving away anything significant.

The night of the operation arrived, draped in a cloak of nervous anticipation. The tension was palpable, a suffocating blanket that weighed heavily on their shoulders. Ghost, a shadowy figure shrouded in a dark coat, materialized as promised in a deserted warehouse near the Thames. His eyes, sharp and calculating, gave away little about his intentions. His expertise was unquestionable, and his methods were as ruthless as they were efficient. At the same time, Benjamin was meticulously breaching the Zurich server's defenses. The cyberattack, executed by Ghost, sent ripples through the European financial system, triggering a wave of panic and frantic response. Every news channel and social media platform was ablaze with reports of the massive cyberattack, diverting the attention away from their real objective.

Cassie watched from a nearby cafe, a silent observer in a sea of chaos. She subtly altered the information she was providing to Finch's handler, planting seeds of doubt and misinformation. She had to be careful, precise. One wrong move, one slip of the tongue, could ruin everything. The pressure was immense.

Time was running out. Benjamin, having skillfully bypassed the server's multiplelayers of security, had finally reached the central database. He navigated through countless files and folders, desperately searching for the information they needed – the names of the true masterminds behind the conspiracy.

Suddenly, an alarm blared, a deafening siren piercing the night. They had been detected. Someone on the other side had noticed the unusual activity. Benjamin had to act quickly, downloading as much information as possible before they were shut down. He managed to grab some crucial files – encrypted messages, bank records, and coded locations – before the system was locked down. The information was tantalizingly close to revealing the identity of the true orchestrators, but there was also a message he'd missed – a warning, a threat. The threat was directed at Cassie. A personal threat, revealing the identity of one of her previous acquaintances; an old enemy. This new revelation turned the whole mission on its head. The stakes were even higher than they'd initially thought.

Benjamin managed to make a safe exit, escaping the scene moments before the Swiss authorities arrived. They were both in grave danger, both as agents of law and order and personally. Their initial success now felt like a hollow victory. They had uncovered a vital piece of the puzzle, but the enemy was now alerted, and the hunt was on, closing in fast. The next move was critical, and time was running out.

The true battle was yet to begin. The desperate gamble had paid off in a way, but the true price was only starting to reveal itself. The lines between their mission and their survival had blurred, and their future hung precariously in the balance. The game was far from over.

CHAPTER 14

Consequences of Betrayal

"As the adrenaline ebbed, Cassie and Benjamin confronted the chilling reality of betrayal within their ranks. In the dim alleyway, every shadow whispered of deceit, and every step forward deepened their entanglement in a treacherous game where survival was uncertain and trust could be fatal."

The adrenaline that had fueled their escape had begun to ebb, replaced by a chilling sense of vulnerability. The alleyway, previously a refuge, now felt like a cage, the shadows whispering threats they couldn't ignore. Finch's confession hung heavy in the air – a double agent within the inner circle of the conspiracy. But who? And what was their next move? The question echoed in the silence between them, a stark reminder of the precarious situation they found themselves in.

Cassie, ever the pragmatist, began to assess the damage. "The leak," she said, her voice low and controlled, "it compromises everything. Our sources, our leads... everything we've worked for these past months is potentially compromised." Benjamin nodded, the grim reality settling upon him. "Not just the investigation, Cassie. Our lives are on the line." He was thinking of his brother, Liam, still embedded within the military network, potentially walking into a trap laid by an enemy they couldn't identify. The risk of exposure was exponentially higher now.

Their immediate priority was damage control. They needed to identify the double agent before they could launch any further offensive strategies. This meant sifting through every contact, every lead, every piece of information they'd gathered, looking for inconsistencies, anomalies, anything that could point towards a traitor. The task was monumental, a needle in a haystack magnified to the scale of a global conspiracy.

The next few days were a blur of frantic activity. Cassie utilized her network of informants, discreetly probing for any whispers of disloyalty, any unusual transactions, any hint of a double-cross. Benjamin, on the other hand,
meticulously reviewed their files, tracing the steps of the investigation, searching for the point where the leak likely originated. They worked independently, yet in perfect synchronicity, their individual strengths complementing each other.

The pressure mounted with each passing hour. The possibility that the leak went far deeper than just one agent loomed over them. What if multiple individuals were working against them? This was a well-oiled machine, and one betrayal meant that their operation had been infiltrated, potentially by multiple moles. The stakes were too high to afford to be optimistic. Then came the first crack. A seemingly insignificant detail, a minor discrepancy in a financial transaction, unearthed by Benjamin's relentless scrutiny. A payment made to a shell company in the Cayman Islands, linked to one of their key informants, a seasoned veteran code-named "Cardinal." Cardinal, a source Benjamin had trusted implicitly, a man whose information had been invaluable.

The revelation hung heavy in the air, a chilling confirmation of their worst fears. Doubt was now not merely a theoretical concept, but a brutal fact. They were not dealing with a single rogue agent, but a network, possibly even an established cell of double agents working in unison. The enemy was closer than they had ever imagined; closer than they dared to contemplate.

Cassie's extensive network had also flagged Cardinal. Her informants painted a picture of a man who had suddenly become inexplicably wealthy, living beyond his means. His lavish lifestyle was a glaring contradiction to his established persona. This wasn't just a matter of a single betrayal, but a sophisticated operation. Their combined analysis pointed towards Cardinal's involvement. The scale of the conspiracy was terrifying. The double agent was not some low-level operative, but a pivotal figure within the clandestine network. His position provided him with access to sensitive information, enabling him to systematically sabotage their investigation. The weight of this betrayal crashed down upon them, a suffocating burden.

They decided to set a trap. A carefully constructed scenario designed to expose Cardinal and uncover the extent of the conspiracy. It was a risky move, a gamble withpotentially catastrophic consequences, but they had no other choice. Their pursuit of justice was now intertwined with their survival. Their own lives had become the stakes in this dangerous game. The trap involved a carefully orchestrated "leak" of false information – a decoy operation designed to lure Cardinal into revealing his true allegiance. The bait was a seemingly insignificant piece of intelligence, laced with subtle contradictions, designed to test his loyalty.

The tension was palpable as they waited, the hours stretching into an eternity. They were playing a deadly game of cat and mouse, knowing that one wrong move could be fatal. The vulnerability was agonizing; they were not dealing with just an agent; they were confronting a well-organized network. Their lives were literally on the line. The consequences of failure were too catastrophic to contemplate. The sense of dread was almost palpable.

The response came swiftly, unexpectedly. Cardinal took the bait, contacting his handlers, revealing his treachery. The information he transmitted confirmed their suspicions – a far-reaching conspiracy involving several high-ranking officials within international organizations. The network was vast and sophisticated, its tendrils reaching deep into the heart of global power. The extent of the betrayal was breathtaking. It was a testament to how well this network was operating and how successful they had been in their campaign to mislead law enforcement.

The trap had worked, but the victory felt hollow. The exposure of Cardinal had only scratched the surface; it had revealed the sheer magnitude of the conspiracy, and the daunting task that still lay ahead. The consequences of the betrayal were far-reaching, their investigations now irrevocably compromised. They had to act swiftly and decisively. The threat was far greater than they had initially anticipated.

The weight of their discovery pressed heavily upon them. The implications were staggering. The conspiracy stretched far beyond their initial expectations, and the danger they now faced was far more insidious and deadly than they could have ever imagined. They needed a plan, a way to dismantle the network before it could inflict any further damage. The task ahead was enormous, a monumental struggle against a vast and powerful enemy. And the enemy was now alerted to their presence and to their knowledge of this massive conspiracy.

Their alliance, already tested, now faced its greatest trial. The lines between hunter and hunted had blurred, and their survival depended on their ability to trust each other completely. Their individual skills and strengths would be tested to their absolute limits. The fight had only just begun, and the stakes were higher than ever. They were in the eye of the storm, their very lives hanging precariously in the balance.

The fight for justice, and for their lives, had just become a whole lot harder. The consequences of the betrayal had plunged them into the darkest depths of this treacherous game, and there was no guarantee of survival.

CHAPTER 15

A Shocking Revelation

"As the London wind howled around them, the revelation of betrayal sliced through Cassie and Benjamin like a knife. Thrust into a deadly game where every ally was a potential enemy, they had to navigate the shadows of a sprawling conspiracy, knowing their next move could be their last."

The biting London wind whipped around them, carrying the scent of rain and the lingering metallic tang of fear. Cassie pulled her coat tighter, the chill seeping into her bones, mirroring the icy dread that had settled in her gut. Finch's confession, a venomous dart aimed at the heart of their operation, had left them reeling. A double agent. The very foundation of their mission, painstakingly built on fragile trust and calculated risks, had crumbled beneath them.

Benjamin, usually a bastion of controlled intensity, was visibly shaken. His normally sharp eyes, usually scanning for threats, were clouded with a turmoil that mirrored her own. The weight of the revelation pressed down on them, heavy and suffocating. Their immediate escape had been a blur of adrenaline and instinct, but now, the silence of the alleyway amplified the enormity of the situation. "We need to go back," Benjamin said, his voice low, almost a growl. The words hung in the air, sharp and decisive, cutting through the silence. His usually calculated demeanor was replaced with an almost desperate urgency.

Cassie hesitated. Going back into the lion's den was reckless, suicidal even. But inaction felt like a slow, agonizing death. The information Finch had provided, however fragmented, was their only lead. It was a thread, thin and fragile, but it was all they had. "No," Cassie replied, her voice equally firm. "Not yet. We need to analyze what we have. Finch's confession was…vague. He didn't name names. He gave us clues, breadcrumbs scattered in the dark." They sought refuge in a nearby pub, the warm, dimly lit interior a stark contrast to the cold, unforgiving alleyway. The comforting aroma of beer and roasted nuts did little to soothe their frayed nerves. Over lukewarm tea, they painstakingly pieced together Finch's confession, searching for hidden meanings and overlooked details.

Finch had spoken of a "shadow organization," a clandestine group pulling the strings from the shadows, manipulating events from afar. He had mentioned a code name – "Seraph." A name that sent a shiver down Cassie's spine. It resonated with a chilling familiarity, a whisper from the edges of her memory. She couldn't place it, but the feeling of unease was palpable.

Benjamin, meanwhile, was meticulously reviewing the intelligence gathered before the hostage situation. He focused on the seemingly insignificant details – a missed call, an unusual transaction, a fleeting glance – searching for anomalies that could point to the double agent's identity. He was a meticulous detective, his mind a complex web of connections and deductions.

Hours melted away as they worked, the pub emptying around them, leaving them alone with their mounting anxieties. The more they delved, the more they realized the depth of the conspiracy. The shadow organization wasn't just involved in the hostage situation; they were pulling the strings in a much larger, more sinister game.

As dawn broke, painting the sky in hues of gray and orange, a chilling realization dawned on Cassie. The seemingly random events, the seemingly unconnected threads, were all part of a larger tapestry. And the pattern was intricate, sinister, and breathtakingly ambitious. "Seraph," she whispered, her voice barely audible above the murmur of the city awakening. "It's... it's not just a code name. It's a person."Benjamin looked up, his eyes widening in understanding. The pieces of the puz zle were falling into place, revealing a picture far more terrifying than they could have imagined. The double agent wasn't just a mole within their team; they were a key player in the shadow organization. And their betrayal ran far deeper than they had ever imagined.

The shocking revelation hit them like a physical blow. It wasn't just one person, but a carefully orchestrated web of deceit. The double agent was someone they trusted implicitly, someone who was deeply embedded within their own inner circle, a person they had worked alongside, potentially sharing sensitive information with. The very foundation of trust that held their operation together was utterly shattered.

The implication was horrifying. Every contact they'd made, every piece of intel shared, every action taken – all of it could have been compromised. The enemy was not just outside, in the shadows, but inside, in plain sight, wearing the guise of an ally. This revelation forced a complete reassessment of their alliances. They were not just hunting for a rogue agent; they were hunting for a viper within their midst. The stakes had just escalated exponentially, plunging them into a treacherous game of cat and mouse where trust was a luxury they could no longer afford.

Their previous alliances felt fragile and untested. The weight of suspicion settled heavy upon them, poisoning every past interaction. The painstakingly constructed trust between Cassie and Benjamin felt suddenly insufficient, inadequate in the face of such widespread deceit. Could they even trust each other entirely, knowing the possibility of a deeper, more insidious betrayal looming?

Their investigation now had to shift dramatically. They needed to go beyond Finch's limited information and explore the connections between the shadow organization and their own inner circle. The hunt for "Seraph" demanded a complete restructuring of their strategy, a relentless pursuit that required not just skill and cunning but an unwavering determination to expose the truth, even if it meant tearing down everything they thought they knew.

The immediate priority was to identify potential suspects within their network. They had to review every past interaction, scrutinizing every conversation, every
exchanged email, every shared moment for any inconsistencies. The task was monumental, a herculean effort to sift through mountains of data, seeking the telltale signs of betrayal. This wasn't just a criminal investigation; it was a psychological chess match, a battle of wits against an unseen adversary who knew their strengths and weaknesses intimately.

Benjamin, leveraging his years of experience in law enforcement, began to systematically eliminate individuals from their list of contacts. His approach was methodical, based on cold, hard facts and evidence. He meticulously analyzed communication patterns, financial records, and even social media activity, looking for anything that could indicate a link to the shadow organization or any deviation from the established norms of behavior.

Cassie, meanwhile, focused on her own network of contacts, leveraging her expertise in negotiation and high-stakes situations. She understood the importance of human psychology, the subtle nuances of body language, and the unspoken cues that could betray a hidden agenda. She re-examined past interactions, searching for any discrepancies, any flicker of hesitation, any subtle shift in loyalty. This intricate game required an understanding of motivations, of the emotional landscape that propelled individuals towards betrayal.

Their joint investigation, while initially fraught with suspicion and the shadow of the recent betrayal, became a necessary collaboration. They were bound together not just by the shared peril but by the determination to expose the conspiracy that threatened global security. The shared mission brought them closer together in the face of overwhelming odds.

The line between hunter and hunted was blurred. Trust had become a scarce commodity, yet their survival hung in the balance on the tenuous thread of their newfound, tested alliance. The revelation had plunged them into the heart of the darkness. The fight for justice, for survival, and for the truth became a relentless pursuit of a shadow that seemed always one step ahead.

The trail of the double agent, now interwoven with the larger conspiracy, led them through a labyrinth of deceit, threatening to consume them at every turn. The journey ahead promised to be treacherous, but the promise of unveiling the truth and bringing "Seraph" to justice fueled their determination. The game was far from over. The hunt had just begun. The stakes were higher than ever before.

CHAPTER 16

Pursuit of the Conspirators

"In the aftermath of the London hostage crisis, the remnants of their shattered world lay before them. As Cassie and Benjamin confronted the twisted web of deception, the shadows of a global conspiracy loomed larger, and their resolve to uncover the truth became a race against an unforgiving clock."

The shattered remnants of the London hostage situation lay scattered like broken glass – a deceptive calm masking the storm still brewing beneath the surface. Cassie, her usually impeccable composure slightly frayed, stared at the grainy CCTV footage, her gaze fixed on the fleeing figures. Three men, their faces obscured by shadows and strategically placed obstacles, melted into the labyrinthine streets of London.

They were the core of the conspiracy, the puppeteers pulling the strings of the elaborate charade. Benjamin, his jaw tight with grim determination, stood beside her, the weight of responsibility heavy on his shoulders. His brother, Dimitri a man carved from granite and honed by years of Navy SEAL training, ran a hand through his close-cropped hair, his usual easy confidence replaced by a simmering intensity. "They're professionals," Dimitri stated, his voice low and gravelly, the words hanging in the air like a threat. "Clean getaway. They knew what they were doing. This wasn't their first rodeo." He pointed to a detail Cassie had missed—a subtle shift in body language, a fleeting glance that revealed a pre-arranged signal. "They had backup. Look at the way they coordinated their escape. This wasn't improvisation; it was a well-rehearsed operation."

Cassie nodded, acknowledging Dimitri's insightful observation. Their initial assessment had been too simplistic. They hadn't anticipated the level of sophistication, the intricate network of support enabling such a seamless escape. The pursuit wouldn't be a simple matter of chasing shadows; it would require meticulous planning, precise execution, and an element of luck. The conspiracy extended far beyond the immediate hostage situation; it was a tangled web woven from deceit, betrayal, and hidden agendas, reaching into the highest echelons of power. The initial London operation was nothing more than a cleverly orchestrated distraction, a smokescreen concealing a much larger, more sinister plan.

Their investigation revealed fragments of information—cryptic messages intercepted from secure servers, coded transmissions hinting at a complex network, and a trail of financial transactions leading to offshore accounts in several tax havens. The trail was deliberately obfuscated, designed to confuse and mislead, to make the pursuit as difficult as possible. Each piece of the puzzle was a challenge, a testament to the conspirators' intelligence and resources. The race was on. Every second counted. Their first lead came from an unexpected source – a disgruntled employee of a seemingly innocuous financial firm with links to several of the offshore accounts. He provided them with a list of names, coded designations, and locations – a roadmap through the maze of the conspiracy, but one fraught with danger.

He revealed a network of shell corporations, phantom businesses existing only on paper, designed to launder money and obscure the true nature of their illicit activities. He spoke of a shadowy organization, known only as "The Obsidian Circle," an entity that operated in the darkness, pulling strings from the shadows, their reach stretching across continents. The information, though valuable, came at a price. The informant, terrified for his life, disappeared without a trace shortly after providing the details. They were running against a clock that was ticking relentlessly. Benjamin's frustration mounted as he realized the depth of the conspiracy, the sheer scale of the operation. They were hunting ghosts, chasing shadows in a world where trust was a rare and precious commodity.

The chase took them from the dimly lit back alleys of London, across the sun-drenched beaches of the Côte d'Azur, and finally to the snow-capped peaks of the Swiss Alps. Each location was a carefully chosen node within the conspiracy's network, each offering a glimpse into the inner workings of the Obsidian Circle. In London, they unearthed encrypted files hidden within seemingly innocent documents; in France, they infiltrated a high-stakes poker game attended by several key players; and in Switzerland, they discovered a hidden vault containing incriminating evidence that could bring down the entire operation.

The pursuit was relentless, a cat-and-mouse game played on a global scale. They faced numerous challenges – near misses with deadly assassins, treacherous terrains that tested their physical and mental endurance, and betrayals that forced them to question the loyalty of those closest to them. Mark's military expertise proved invaluable, allowing them to navigate treacherous situations and outwit their pursuers.

Cassie's negotiation skills were put to the test, not just in dealing with the conspirators but also in navigating the
complex political landscape, securing assistance from unexpected allies. Benjamin's detective skills, his sharp mind capable of dissecting intricate details, helped them connect the dots and uncover the truth. Their journey wasn't without casualties. Trust was a fragile thing, easily shattered by betrayal. They faced

moments of doubt, questioning their decisions, their alliances, and eventheir own sanity. The psychological pressure was immense, constantly gnawing at their resolve.

The conspirators were masters of manipulation, using fear and intimidation to control and silence their opponents. The line between friend and foe blurred as they uncovered hidden agendas and shifted allegiances, leaving them constantly on guard, questioning everyone's motives. Every contact, every piece of information, needed careful scrutiny. During their perilous journey, they forged unlikely alliances. A disillusioned former member of The Obsidian Circle, haunted by his past, offered crucial information in exchange for immunity. A seasoned journalist, initially skeptical, became an invaluable ally, providing vital insights and disseminating information through carefully chosen channels. These unexpected partnerships became crucial in their fight against a formidable adversary.

The final confrontation took place in a remote Alpine villa, a breathtakingly beautiful location that served as a chilling contrast to the grim reality of the situation. The mastermind, a figure whose identity had remained shrouded in mystery until now, was revealed to be someone they had previously encountered, someone they had once trusted. The revelation was a crushing blow, shattering their assumptions and forcing them to confront the depths of human deception. The showdown was a brutal dance of wits and skill, a deadly ballet played out against the backdrop of a breathtaking landscape. Dimitri's military training proved crucial, his precision and efficiency providing the edge they desperately needed.

Cassie's negotiation tactics, refined over years of experience, helped them outmaneuver the mastermind, exposing their flaws and leveraging their weaknesses. Benjamin's keen observation skills proved invaluable in identifying crucial details that turned the tide of the battle. The confrontation was a battle of attrition, a relentless test of courage and resilience, ultimately ending with the mastermind's capture. Their victory, however, came at a price.

The experience left its mark on them all, their physical and emotional scars a testament to the intensity of the pursuit. They had stared into the abyss and emerged battered, but not broken.

The Obsidian Circle was dismantled, but the experience left them forever changed, the cost of justice etched onto their souls. The uneasy alliance forged in the fires of the London hostage situation had blossomed into something more profound, a bond forged in the crucible of shared danger and unwavering determination. They had faced the shadows and emerged, bruised but stronger, ready to face whatever the future held. Their journey had just begun.

CHAPTER 17

A Perilous Journey

"In the dim glow of the CCTV footage, Cassie, Benjamin, and Dimitri glimpsed the tangled web of a sinister scheme. As they plunged deeper into the labyrinth of deception, the lines between hunter and hunted blurred, revealing a conspiracy that stretched across continents and penetrated the highest echelons of power."

The grainy CCTV footage offered little more than frustrating glimpses of their quarry. The three men, their identities still shrouded in mystery, moved with a practiced ease that spoke of extensive training and meticulous planning. They were ghosts, flitting through the crowded streets of London, disappearing as quickly as they appeared, leaving behind only the echo of their audacity. Benjamin, his eyes narrowed in concentration, pointed to a fleeting image on the screen. "That's a distinctive gait," he murmured, his voice low and gravelly. "I've seen that before." Cassie, her mind already racing ahead, leaned closer. "Where?"

"A surveillance video from a previous operation," he replied, a flicker of recognition in his eyes. "It was an art heist, years ago. The same style, the same calculated movements. These guys are professionals." The realization hit Cassie with the force of a physical blow. This wasn't just a random act of terrorism; it was part of a larger, more sinister scheme, orchestrated by a network of highly skilled operatives. The Obsidian Circle, they had called it in London. But this was different; this felt…bigger.

Dimitri, ever the pragmatist, broke the silence. "We need to trace their movements. Interpol might have something, but we need to be quicker. Their trail could go cold at any moment." He pulled out his satellite phone, the hum of the device cutting through the tense atmosphere. His connections ran deeper than anyone's, a network built through years of service and unwavering loyalty. He spoke in hushed tones, his voice sharp and precise, commanding attention. The information that followed confirmed their worst fears. The three men had vanished into the international underworld, their movements carefully obscured, like ripples disappearing into a vast, dark ocean.

They were headed east, their destination unknown, their trail fragmented and deliberately misleading. This wasn't a simple criminal investigation anymore; it had become a high-stakes game of cat and mouse, played across continents and across clandestine networks. The stakes were impossibly high, and the players were ruthless. Their journey began in a small, nondescript office in Amsterdam, a city shrouded in secrets and shadowed by the long arms of powerful clandestine organizations. The air hung heavy with the scent of coffee and anticipation as Cassie and Benjamin, joined by Dimitri, pored over the data. Dimitri's contacts had managed to locate a fleeting financial transaction, a sum of money transferred through a series of shell corporations, ultimately leading them to a shadowy figure operating out of Prague. This man, they believed, was the key, the conduit between the three fugitives and the larger network.

Their travel plans were swift and clandestine, employing a series of private jets and secure ground transportation. Their routes were deliberately complex, designed to throw off any potential pursuers. Their identities remained masked, their movements shadowed by a team of skilled operatives working in the background, each playing their role in this dangerous ballet of deception. Prague offered a chilling contrast to the bright lights of London, its cobbled streets and gothic architecture whispering stories of long-forgotten conspiracies. The city felt heavy with secrets, its atmosphere thick with an unspoken tension.

The man they sought, a cold-blooded operative named Anton Volkov, operated from a seemingly innocuous gallery, a facade concealing a sophisticated network of criminal activities. He was a master of disguise, a chameleon who changed his identity with each passing transaction. He was a puppet master, pulling the strings of this international game, his actions veiled by a network of aliases and offshore accounts. The information they possessed was scant, but it was enough. It was a puzzle, and they were determined to solve it. Cassie, as the lead negotiator, had planned a subtle approach, her tactics honed through years of experience.

They would attempt to gain Volkov's trust, playing on his weaknesses, exploiting his vulnerabilities, and carefully extracting the information they needed. It was a high-stakes gamble, but they had no other choice. Benjamin, with his instinctive grasp of criminal psychology, would provide crucial insights, interpreting subtle cues and anticipating Volkov's next move. Dimitri, with his military background, was providing the muscle, their silent protector, a grim guardian angel in the shadows.

Their days in Prague were a tense blend of surveillance and strategic planning. They tracked Volkov's movements, observing his interactions, piecing together the fragments of his life. They learned about his fondness for expensive art, his meticulous attention to detail, and his ruthless efficiency. He was a man who lived on the edge, always one step ahead, constantly shifting the ground beneath his feet.

The gallery itself was a labyrinth of deception, its walls adorned with seemingly harmless paintings, each one potentially concealing a hidden message, a coded communication, a secret rendezvous point. The air was thick with the scent of old wood and expensive perfume, a strange position of beauty and menace. The tension in the air was palpable, each moment pregnant with possibility.

Finally, the opportunity presented itself. Volkov, lured by a meticulously crafted proposition involving a rare piece of art, arrived at a secluded meeting room within the gallery. Cassie, armed with her unwavering composure, initiated the negotiation, her voice calm and measured, her words carefully chosen. She played the part of a wealthy art collector, her eyes betraying no emotion, her body language controlled and deliberate.

The exchange was fraught with tension. Volkov, his eyes sharp and calculating, was wary but intrigued. He tested her, probing her for weaknesses, searching for any hint of
deception. Cassie, in turn, played him skillfully, dropping hints, carefully guiding the conversation, gradually drawing him out, unraveling his carefully constructed facade. The minutes stretched into an eternity, the silence filled with unspoken threats and veiled promises.

It was during a momentary lapse in his guard that Benjamin spotted it – a subtle flicker in Volkov's eyes, a micro-
expression that betrayed his true intentions. He signaled to Dimitri, his eyes conveying a silent command. The element of surprise was critical; failure meant jeopardizing the entire operation. The risk was significant, but they were prepared for anything.

Dimitri moved with the speed and precision of a highly trained operative, his presence a force to be reckoned with. The transition was seamless, swift, and decisive. Volkov, caught off guard, realized the truth. He was outmatched, his carefully laid plans crumbling around him. The game was over. Cassie, having secured the crucial information, maintained her calm demeanor, but her heart was pounding in her chest.

The information they extracted from Volkov proved to be the missing piece of the puzzle, revealing the true scope of the conspiracy. It was a network far more extensive and dangerous than they had initially imagined, a global
organization with deep roots in the international underworld. They were not just dealing with criminals; they were dealing with shadowy figures operating with impunity, their reach extending into governments and corporations, their motives shrouded in secrecy.

The chase was far from over; it had just taken a dangerous new turn. Their journey had led them from the chaotic streets of London to the dark heart of a complex international conspiracy. The world, it seemed, was far more dangerous than they had ever imagined. Their journey had only just begun.

CHAPTER 18

Unexpected Challenges

"From the covert shadows of London's alleys to the strategic vantage points of the French Riviera, Cassie, Benjamin, and Dimitri advanced their mission with unwavering resolve. The line between ally and adversary blurred as the scale of the conspiracy unfolded, testing their tactical precision and the honor bound by their duty."

The chase led them from the dimly lit back alleys of London to the sun-drenched shores of the French Riviera. The trail, initially a faint whisper, had solidified into a tangible pursuit, thanks to a contact in Interpol – a gruff, chain-smoking woman named Isabelle Moreau who owed Benjamin a considerable debt. Moreau's information pinpointed the next likely rendezvous point for their elusive targets: a secluded villa overlooking the azure waters of the Mediterranean.

The villa, a sprawling white monstrosity with manicured gardens and a private beach, was the epitome of discreet luxury. It was the kind of place where secrets were whispered, deals were struck, and identities were carefully concealed behind a veneer of sophistication. Benjamin and Cassie arrived under the cover of darkness, their approach cautious and deliberate. They had learned theirlesson in London – underestimating their opponents was a fatal mistake.

Their plan was simple, yet fraught with peril: surveillance. They needed to observe the comings and goings, identify the key players, and determine the nature of their operation. But even the seemingly straightforward task of surveillance proved to be more challenging than anticipated. The villa was heavily fortified, guarded by men who moved with the practiced efficiency of seasoned professionals. Their security systems were state-of-the-art, and their vigilance relentless.

Cassie, using her considerable negotiation skills and a meticulously crafted cover story, managed to infiltrate the outer perimeter of the estate, posing as a high-end real estate agent interested in purchasing the property. She charmed her way past the initial security checkpoints, her wit and charisma deflecting suspicion. Meanwhile, Benjamin, with the help of a local contact, secured a vantage point overlooking the villa from a nearby cliff face. Their communication was discreet, relying on encrypted channels and pre-arranged hand signals.

Their initial observations were unsettling. The men they had been tracking were meeting with individuals who appeared to be high-ranking officials from various governments and corporations. The conversations were hushed, secretive, but snippets of information gleaned through careful listening painted a disturbing picture. It was far more than a simple criminal enterprise; it was a conspiracy of global proportions, threatening to destabilize international relations and potentially spark a major conflict.

The first unexpected challenge arose in the form of a sudden power outage. The villa's sophisticated security system, reliant on constant power, went dark, plunging the entire estate into chaos. This seemingly random event was likely no coincidence. Their opponents were aware of their presence, and this was their way of disrupting their surveillance. The darkness forced Cassie to abandon her cover and retreat.

Benjamin, on the cliff, watched as chaos erupted. The guards scrambled, their movements frantic and disorganized in the sudden darkness. It was the perfect opportunity to strike, but he knew he couldn't risk a frontal assault. He was outnumbered and outgunned. He needed a backup plan. He contacted his brother, Dimitri the Navy SEAL, who was already en route.

Dimitri's arrival brought a welcome surge of military precision. He assessed the situation quickly, proposing a daring plan: a coordinated attack utilizing specialized equipment and utilizing the cover of darkness to their advantage. Dimitri's plan relied on a precise understanding of the villa's layout and security protocols, knowledge that was hard-won through painstaking research and high-level military intel.

But even with Dimitri's expertise, the operation proved far riskier than anticipated. The villa's security proved far more robust than their initial reconnaissance suggested. Hidden cameras, motion sensors, and pressure plates made their approach perilous. They faced multiple near misses, each a stark reminder of the danger they were in. Several times, they were almost discovered. Their close call with detection forced them to adapt their strategy, improvise, and rely on their years of training to navigate the hostile environment.

Another significant challenge presented itself in the form of unforeseen reinforcements. A heavily armed private military contractor arrived at the villa, seemingly out of nowhere. Their arrival completely changed the equation. This added a layer of complexity to an already dangerous situation. These mercenaries were highly trained, well-equipped, and their loyalty was not easily questioned, making any attempt at infiltration that much more risky.

The unexpected arrival of the mercenaries forced a complete rethink of the mission. The original plan was now completely obsolete. The risk of a full-scale confrontation was too high. Their initial objective of surveillance shifted to a focus on gathering intel and assessing their opponent's capabilities to inform their next move.

Cassie, using her unique skills in negotiation, attempted to contact one of the mercenaries, a man named Antonov, through a coded message delivered via a seemingly innocuous courier. Her message suggested a potential business opportunity that was too good to refuse, but
Antonov was initially skeptical. Cassie played the long game, slowly building trust, offering tantalizing glimpses of a lucrative side deal, and highlighting the risks of continued collaboration with their current employers.

The negotiation was excruciatingly slow, a delicate dance of deceit and persuasion. Cassie had to play on Antonov's greed and ambition, exploiting his desire for a better life, while simultaneously making him feel secure and indispensable. It was a gamble, one that could easily backfire. She played it cool, masking her nervousness behind an air of confidence and professionalism.

Antonov's ultimate defection to their side changed everything. He provided valuable insights into the inner workings of the operation, revealing the identities of the key players, and giving them access to internal communications. He even provided a detailed floor plan of the villa. This invaluable intelligence gave them a significant edge. Their previous disadvantage now turned to their advantage.

With Antonov's help, Benjamin and Dimitri developed a new plan, a more surgical approach that focused on infiltration rather than a direct confrontation. Their updated mission now shifted to extracting key evidence to expose the conspiracy. This evidence would be enough to take down the entire operation, crippling the organization and bringing its leaders to justice. The focus moved from a full-scale assault to a delicate extraction of critical information. The operation was incredibly risky. Each step was fraught with potential pitfalls. One wrong move could expose them, leading to dire consequences. Their lives hung in the balance.

The final stage of their operation involved a daring infiltration of the villa's main server room. Working under the cover of a simulated power outage, which Antonov triggered from the inside, Benjamin and Dimitri moved
through the darkened corridors of the villa, using their knowledge of the layout and the distraction created by the planned power cut. Cassie meanwhile, secured a diversion by engaging a secondary security detail in a distracting yet harmless standoff, using her advanced negotiation tactics to buy them time.

In the server room, Benjamin accessed the organization's encrypted database, successfully downloading terabytes of incriminating data. They quickly realized that the true scope of the conspiracy went far beyond anything they had initially imagined. The data revealed a complex network of influence, corruption, and deceit extending into the highest echelons of global power. The stakes were higher than ever. This was no longer just about rescuing hostages; it was about preventing global catastrophe.

Their escape from the villa was a tense and perilous affair, a harrowing race against time. They had to move quickly and quietly, navigating the labyrinthine corridors, evading any remaining guards. The adrenaline pumped through their veins, fueling their every movement. They had to remain on high alert; any complacency could be fatal. Their success hinged on perfect coordination, perfect execution, and a little bit of luck. With Antonov providing critical inside information and support, they made it out alive.

They left the villa behind, leaving the chaos of their infiltration in their wake, carrying with them the evidence that would expose a dangerous conspiracy and its powerful architects. But their work was far from over. The data theyhad secured represented a significant victory, but it also laid bare the terrifying truth about the global reach and influence of their opponents. The chase had just begun anew, on a larger and far more dangerous scale. The true fight had only just begun.

CHAPTER 19

Strategic Alliances

"From the rugged paths of the Swiss Alps, Cassie, Benjamin, and Dimitri pressed forward with unwavering resolve. As they uncovered the layers of a vast conspiracy, questions arose: How deep did this network run, and who were the hidden puppeteers behind it all?"

The battered Land Rover, its tires spitting gravel, climbed the winding mountain road. Inside, Cassie gripped the worn leather seat, her knuckles white. Benjamin, beside her, stared intently at the GPS, his jaw tight. The data Antonov had provided – a fragmented, encrypted file detailing the conspiracy's global network – led them to this remote location in the Swiss Alps: a seemingly innocuous research facility nestled amongst snow-capped peaks. This wasn't just about a stolen bioweapon anymore; it was about a vast, meticulously planned operation that threatened to destabilize the entire world order. The sheer scale of it was staggering.

Their initial pursuit had been a frantic chase, a desperate attempt to stay one step ahead of their adversaries. Now, the chase had morphed into something far more calculated, requiring strategy, precision, and a network of unlikely allies. Antonov, their unexpected lifeline from the villa, had provided more than just the encrypted data; he'd offered access to his own network, a shadowy group of former intelligence operatives operating outside the law. These individuals, once enemies, were now their only hope.

Their first contact was a woman named Anya Volkov, a former KGB agent with icy blue eyes and a reputation as lethal as it was enigmatic. She met them in a secluded chalet, the air thick with the scent of pine and secrecy. Anya, her face impassive, handed Cassie a small, intricately carved wooden box. Inside lay a microchip, containing a crucial piece of the puzzle – a list of names, locations, and dates detailing the conspiracy's financial transactions and logistical support networks. The list revealed a spiderweb of shell corporations, offshore accounts, and shadowy facilitators, reaching into every corner of the globe. "This is only a fraction," Anya stated, her voice low and controlled, her gaze unwavering. "But it's enough to unravel the entire operation. The key is to expose their funding. Cut off the money, and you cripple the snake."

Anya's expertise was invaluable. She spoke of laundering techniques so sophisticated, so well-hidden, they were virtually untraceable. But she knew the players involved, understood their methods, and possessed the contacts to expose their intricate financial maneuvers. She offered Cassie and Benjamin access to her network of financial analysts, hackers, and investigative journalists who specialized in uncovering this kind of deep-rooted corruption.

Their next move involved forging an alliance with a highly unlikely player: General Omar Khan, a former Pakistani military intelligence officer, now living in self-imposed exile in Dubai. Khan, once a staunch opponent of Western interests, had recently experienced a radical shift in allegiance, fueled by a deep-seated disillusionment with the very organization he once served. He possessed unparalleled knowledge of the inner workings of the conspiracy's operations in the Middle East and South Asia.

The meeting took place in a dimly lit hookah lounge, the air heavy with the scent of exotic spices and anticipation. Negotiations were tense, fueled by mutual distrust and suspicion. Benjamin, relying on his honed interrogation skills, patiently chipped away at Khan's reservations, revealing just enough information to pique the general's interest, while carefully maintaining a delicate balance of power. Cassie, employing her expertise in negotiation, eased the tensions and navigated the cultural complexities of the conversation, emphasizing the shared threat to global stability.

Khan's contribution was invaluable; he provided the missing link connecting the disparate elements of the conspiracy. He revealed the involvement of a clandestine organization known only as "The Obsidian Hand," a shadowy group with ties to several rogue states and extremist factions. The Obsidian Hand's objective was not merely financial gain; they aimed to destabilize global politics, creating a power vacuum that could be exploited for their own nefarious purposes. Their plan was audacious, terrifying in its scope.

As they delved deeper into the investigation, the risks escalated exponentially. They weren't just up against a group of criminals; they were facing a well-organized, highly sophisticated network with global reach and influence. They faced the constant threat of betrayal, sabotage, and assassination. Every phone call, every meeting, every piece of information gathered risked exposing them to their enemies.

Benjamin's twin brother, Dimitri, a Navy SEAL with an elite counter-terrorism unit, was brought into the fold. Dimitrioffered invaluable tactical support, his expertise in covert operations and military strategies crucial in navigating the perilous path ahead. His knowledge of advanced surveillance techniques and counter-surveillance measures proved invaluable, allowing them to remain one step ahead of their pursuers.

Their alliance, however, was not without its challenges. The clash of personalities, the differences in operational style, the inherent distrust between law enforcement, intelligence agencies, and the military created constant friction. Cassie, accustomed to navigating delicate diplomatic negotiations, found herself grappling with the hard-nosed, uncompromising tactics of the military. Benjamin, ever the pragmatist, had to find common ground between his brother's military precision and Cassie's nuanced approach.

Despite these challenges, they forged a functional alliance –a fragile pact born out of necessity and a shared sense of purpose. They realized they were fighting a war against a powerful enemy, a war that demanded collaboration, mutual trust, and unwavering resolve. Their success depended on their ability to overcome their differences, to leverage their diverse skills, and to trust each other implicitly. The stakes were too high to fail. The world hung in the balance.

Their next step involved infiltrating a heavily guarded summit in Geneva, a high-profile gathering of world leaders and influential figures. The Obsidian Hand was planning to exploit this summit, using it as a platform to launch a series of coordinated attacks designed to create chaos and further destabilize the world order. Stopping them required a carefully orchestrated operation, requiring the combined expertise of their diverse alliance. The odds were stacked against them, the risks immense, but they were prepared to do whatever it took to expose the conspiracy and bring those responsible to justice.

The chase continued, leading them into a labyrinthine world of international intrigue, betrayal, and unexpected alliances, where the lines between friend and foe blurred, and survival depended on making the right choices. The fight was far from over, and the true test of their alliance lay ahead. The world held its breath.

CHAPTER 20

A Confrontation

"As Cassie, Benjamin, and Dimitri delved deeper into the shadows of the conspiracy, each discovery revealed more layers of deception. Their path, fraught with danger, demanded not only their skill but also the courage to confront the darkest corners of global power."

The Land Rover lurched violently as Benjamin wrestled with the steering wheel, navigating a treacherous hairpin bend. The snow, heavy and relentless, obscured the already precarious road. Cassie, her breath misting in the frigid air, watched the GPS tracker anxiously. The signal, faint but persistent, indicated their target was close. The research facility, a monolithic structure of brutalist concrete and steel, loomed ahead, its stark silhouette piercing the swirling snow. It was a fortress, seemingly impervious to attack, its defenses layered and impenetrable."This is it," Benjamin muttered, his voice tight with anticipation. "Antonov's intel was right. This place… this is where they're coordinating everything."

Cassie nodded, her gaze fixed on the facility's imposing structure. "But how do we get in? This place is a military installation, disguised as a research center." She ran a hand through her hair, the adrenaline pumping through her veins. The air crackled with tension, the silence punctuated only by the roar of the engine and the howling wind. Their plan was audacious, bordering on suicidal. They wouldn't be able to breach the facility's perimeter undetected. Their only hope was to exploit a vulnerability, a weakness in the system. Antonov's fragmented data had alluded to a clandestine entrance, a hidden passage used for covert operations. Finding it was their first hurdle.

They parked the Land Rover behind a snowdrift, camouflaging it effectively. The wind whipped around them, biting at their exposed skin. Benjamin checked his weapons, a suppressed pistol holstered at his hip, a tactical knife strapped to his thigh. Cassie, equally armed, ran through their infiltration plan one last time. They moved with practiced precision, their movements fluid and silent. The approach was nerve-wracking. Cameras, sensors, and armed guards patrolled the perimeter. They moved like ghosts, their every step measured and deliberate, utilizing the shadows and the swirling snow to their advantage.

Benjamin's knowledge of military tactics proved invaluable, guiding them through a labyrinth of fences, surveillance systems, and patrol routes. Finally, after what felt like an eternity, they found it – a small, almost imperceptible opening in the snow-covered embankment near the back of the facility. The entrance led to a narrow, dimly lit tunnel. The air inside was thick with the smell of damp earth and something else, something metallic and faintly acrid. They moved slowly, their senses heightened, their weapons ready. The tunnel seemed to stretch on forever, a claustrophobic passage into the heart of the enemy's lair. Suddenly, a harsh light filled the tunnel. They were discovered.

Two guards, armed with submachine guns, emerged from the darkness, their faces grim. A tense standoff ensued, the air thick with the metallic scent of fear. Benjamin moved swiftly, his movements precise and lethal. He disarmed one guard with a lightning-fast kick, the impact sending the man sprawling to the ground. Cassie reacted simultaneously, her training kicking in as she neutralized the other guard with a well-placed strike to the pressure point in his neck. They moved on, their hearts pounding, the adrenaline coursing through their bodies.

The tunnel opened into a vast underground complex. The scale of the operation was even more staggering than they had anticipated. Rows upon rows of sophisticated equipment lined the walls, humming with silent energy. Computer terminals displayed complex data streams, cryptic symbols flashing across the screens. They had stumbled upon the Obsidian Hand's nerve center.

They navigated the labyrinthine corridors, their every step echoing in the vast underground space. They came across numerous guards, all efficiently dispatched with surgical precision. They were close. They sensed it. The tension ratcheted up a notch. They knew their objective was near. They finally reached a large, reinforced door, heavily guarded. Behind it, they knew, lay their target: Dr. Anya Volkov, the mastermind behind the Obsidian Hand and the architect of the global conspiracy.

The confrontation was inevitable. The guards, alerted to their presence, swarmed them. A ferocious firefight erupted, the air filled with the deafening roar of gunfire and the shattering of glass. Benjamin and Cassie fought back-to-back, their movements coordinated, their skills honed to perfection. They moved with lethal efficiency, their training enabling them to survive the hail of bullets. Despite their superior firepower, the guards were no match for Benjamin and Cassie's combined expertise. One by one, they fell, their bodies crumpling to the ground. Finally, silence descended, broken only by the heavy gasps of their breaths and the rhythmic thump of their hearts. They had won the initial battle. But the true fight was still ahead.

They cautiously opened the reinforced door, their weapons trained on the room beyond. Dr. Volkov was there, seated at a large desk, her face composed, her eyes cold and calculating. She was surrounded by monitors, displaying live feeds from around the globe, showcasing the meticulous planning of the Obsidian Hand's global operation. "Impressive," she said, her voice calm and devoid of emotion. "You've gotten this far. But you can't stop us. The damage is already done. The world is on the brink of chaos, and there's nothing you can do to prevent it."

Benjamin stepped forward, his face grim. "We'll see about that." Cassie studied Volkov's expression, searching for any sign of weakness, any crack in her composure. She knew they had to get information out of her, information that could help them neutralize the threat before it was too late. It was a high-stakes game of wits, a battle of minds. The room hung heavy with the unspoken threat of what was to come. The confrontation had begun. The fate of the world hung precariously in the balance. The quiet hum of the computers seemed to mock their desperate attempt to avert catastrophe. The countdown had begun.

The air crackled with anticipation, the silence punctuated only by the faint ticking of a clock somewhere in the vast complex, marking the dwindling seconds. Dr. Volkov smiled, a chilling, almost imperceptible twitch of her lips. This was only the beginning. The true battle, the fight for the world's future, was about to commence. The tension hung thick and heavy, each breath a calculated risk in a game of ultimate stakes. The quiet hum of the facility's machinery seemed to pulse in rhythm with the frantic beating of their hearts. The world held its breath.

CHAPTER 21

Unmasking the Mastermind

"In the dimly lit interrogation room, the air was thick with unspoken tension. As Cassie and Benjamin unraveled the final threads of the conspiracy, the realization of a personal betrayal hit with devastating force. Their pursuit for justice had led them to this moment, where loyalty and revenge collided in a brutal test of wills."

The air in the dimly lit interrogation room hung heavy with unspoken tension. Cassie, her usual composure subtly frayed, watched as the suspect, a seemingly unremarkable mid-level bureaucrat named Anton Volkov, fidgeted under the harsh glare of the single overhead bulb. Benjamin, his jaw clenched, leaned against the wall, the weight of the past few weeks etched onto his face. Their relentless pursuit had led them down a rabbit hole of deception, betrayal, and close calls, all culminating in this moment. The pieces of the puzzle, scattered across continents and hidden in layers of encrypted communications, were finally beginning to coalesce.

Volkov, despite his attempts at maintaining an air of nonchalance, was cracking. The relentless questioning, the subtle psychological pressure exerted by Cassie, and the unwavering gaze of Benjamin had worn him down. He'd revealed snippets of information – coded phrases, cryptic locations, names whispered like dark secrets – all pointing towards a single, chilling truth. The conspiracy wasn't just about money, power, or even global destabilization; it was personal. It was a meticulously crafted revenge plot, decades in the making.

The mastermind wasn't some shadowy figure pulling strings from a hidden bunker; it was someone they knew, someone they had initially dismissed as a minor player. Someone far closer to Benjamin than they ever could have imagined. The revelation hit Benjamin like a physical blow, a gutwrenching realization that sent a chill down his spine. His brother, Dimitri, the decorated Navy SEAL, the man he'd always looked up to, the man who'd shared his life since birth – Dimitril was the architect of this intricate web of deceit.

The evidence was overwhelming, a carefully constructed tapestry of lies woven with meticulous precision. Dimitri's seemingly innocuous actions, his sudden disappearances, his conveniently timed absences – they were all part of the plan. He'd used his position, his access, his trust, to meticulously orchestrate a series of events designed to cause chaos and reap vengeance. The London hostage situation had been a carefully staged distraction, a bloody sideshow designed to draw attention away from the true scope of his operation.

Cassie, ever the pragmatist, pieced together the details. Dimitri's resentment towards the organization that had framed their father years ago, resulting in his untimely death, fueled his actions. He'd spent years infiltrating the organization, climbing the ranks, patiently waiting for the perfect opportunity to strike. The hostage crisis served as a diversion, while his true aim was far more ambitious: the theft of a highly classified piece of technology capable of crippling global financial markets. The technology, codenamed "Project Chimera," was designed to create instability and chaos on a scale never before witnessed. His motives, though twisted and fueled by revenge, were undeniably personal.

The realization struck Benjamin with the force of a tidal wave. He had trusted his brother implicitly, a bond forged in shared childhood experiences, reinforced by years of mutual support and respect. Now, that trust was shattered, replaced by a nauseating mixture of betrayal, anger, and grief. The weight of the situation pressed down on him, the conflicting emotions threatening to overwhelm him.

The interrogation continued late into the night. Volkov, his spirit broken, revealed the final pieces of the puzzle: the location of Project Chimera, the network of Dimitri's
accomplices, and the intricate mechanism behind the conspiracy's trigger mechanism. Cassie, with her years of experience negotiating with terrorists and criminals, meticulously extracted information, each word carefully weighed and analyzed. She noticed the inconsistencies, the subtle shifts in Volkov's demeanor, the carefully constructed lies designed to protect Dimitri.

The information they gleaned painted a chilling picture of Dimitri's meticulous planning. He had carefully cultivated relationships with seemingly unrelated individuals, each playing a vital role in his grand design. He'd manipulated situations, planted false leads, and used his knowledge of international espionage techniques to cover his tracks. The depth of his deception was staggering, a testament to his intelligence, skill, and ruthless determination.

With the location of Project Chimera identified – a hidden server farm in a remote location in the Swiss Alps – Cassie and Benjamin, along with a small, highly specialized task force, initiated a covert operation to recover the technology. The stakes were impossibly high, failure meaning catastrophic global consequences. Dimitri, meanwhile, was alerted to their move, and a tense cat-and-mouse game ensued, a deadly dance between siblings across the picturesque Swiss landscape.

The climax took place within the heart of the server farm, a sterile environment filled with humming servers and the low thrum of powerful computers. The confrontation between Benjamin and Dimitri was raw, visceral, devoid of pleasantries. It was a brutal clash of ideologies, fueled by years of shared history and a chasm of mutual betrayal. Their bond, once unbreakable, was shattered beyond repair. The fight was intense, each blow carrying the weight of years of unspoken resentment, of broken trust, and the pain of a familial betrayal that tore at the very fabric of their being.

Cassie, despite her experience in such high-stakes situations, was caught off guard by the sheer intensity of the emotional turmoil. She watched, her heart pounding, as the two brothers wrestled, each fueled by vengeance and the desperation of their situation. Benjamin fought with the raw emotion of a man betrayed, his strikes fierce and fueled by grief. Dimitri, cold and calculating, fought with the precision of a seasoned soldier, his movements precise and deadly.

The conflict concluded not with a decisive victory, but with a desperate compromise. Dimitri, cornered and realizing the futility of his actions, agreed to relinquish Project Chimera, but only under the condition that Benjamin promised to look into the circumstances of their father's death, promising to expose the true culprits responsible. The victory was pyrrhic. While Project Chimera was secured, preventing a global catastrophe, the brothers were irrevocably separated, their relationship irreparably damaged.

The aftermath was a complicated tapestry of lingering emotions. While justice had been served, the cost had been significant. The emotional toll on Benjamin was immense, the betrayal by his twin brother leaving an enduring wound. Cassie, though emotionally removed, was deeply affected by the events, witnessing firsthand the devastating power of revenge and the irreparable damage it can cause. The operation's success, while preventing a global crisis, failed to address the deeper issues – the unresolved grief over their father's death and the irreconcilable differences between Benjamin and Dimitri.

The operation's success, while preventing a global financial crisis, left a haunting silence. Project Chimera was secured, but the scars of betrayal ran deeper than any algorithm could ever decipher. The conspiracy was dismantled, yet the brothers' fractured relationship was a constant reminder of the human cost of revenge and the complex interplay of loyalty and betrayal.

The world was safe, for now, but the shadow of their past, and the haunting weight of what could have been, remained. The future held uncertainty, but one thing was certain: Cassie and Benjamin's uneasy alliance, forged in the fires of crisis, would continue to be tested, a testament to the enduring human need for justice, even when justice comes at such a devastating personal cost.

CHAPTER 22

The Master Plan

"In the aftermath of their high-stakes operation, Cassie, Benjamin, and Dimitri faced the reality of their fragile victory. The shadows of the conspiracy still lingered, and as new threats emerged, their resolve was tested once more in a relentless pursuit of justice."

The interrogation yielded little beyond Volkov's carefully constructed denials. He knew nothing, he claimed, about the organization beyond his own limited role in facilitating offshore transactions. His eyes, however, betrayed a flicker of fear whenever Benjamin's twin brother, Dimitri entered the room. Dimitri, a Navy SEAL with a reputation for unconventional methods, had been brought in to provide a different kind of pressure. His presence alone spoke volumes; a silent threat that hung heavier than any verbal accusation.

Cassie, observing the subtle interplay between the brothers –the shared history etched in the subtle tension between them– began to see a pattern. Volkov wasn't lying about his direct involvement, but he was certainly concealing something larger, something far more sinister. This wasn't just about money laundering; this was the tip of a far larger iceberg. Days blurred into nights as they delved deeper, piecing together fragmented information from intercepted communications, recovered documents, and cryptic clues gleaned from Volkov's reluctant confessions. The picture that emerged was terrifyingly intricate, a web of deceit spun across multiple continents, involving powerful players who operated in the shadows.

At the heart of it all was a man named Julian Thorne. Not a name known to the public, Thorne's influence stretched across the global financial landscape, his tentacles wrapped around banks, corporations, and even governments. He wasn't a flashy mastermind; his power was insidious, his methods subtle, but devastatingly effective. Thorne wasn't interested in direct control; his goal was something far more insidious: chaos. He was a puppeteer, pulling strings from the shadows, orchestrating events that would destabilize the global economy, creating an environment of pandemonium where he could seize control.

Thorne's "master plan," as Cassie began to call it, wasn't some grand scheme for world domination. It was far more insidious. He aimed to trigger a cascade of financial collapses, utilizing a complex network of shell corporations and encrypted accounts to move billions of dollars undetected. These transactions weren't simply about stealing money; they were designed to cripple nations, to force governments to their knees, and ultimately, to create a void of power that he could fill.

The method was chillingly simple yet impossibly complex. It involved exploiting vulnerabilities in the international financial system, leveraging the interconnectedness of global markets to magnify the impact of his actions. He had spent years building this network, meticulously weaving his threads into the fabric of the global economy. Each seemingly unrelated event, each minor financial hiccup, was a carefully orchestrated step in his grand design. The collapse of smaller banks, the sudden devaluation of currencies, the widespread panic in the markets—these were all part of his plan.

The pieces of the puzzle finally clicked into place. The seemingly random acts of sabotage, the mysterious disappearances, the encrypted communications all were carefully coordinated pieces of Thorne's grand game. The hostage situation in London, the seemingly unrelated financial crimes, the political unrest in several key regions -they were all meticulously planned to weaken global stability and create an environment of chaos where Thorne could emerge as the savior, the one man with the solution.

But Thorne's ambition had blinded him to a crucial flaw: his underestimation of Cassie and Benjamin's dogged determination. Their investigation, initially focused on a relatively minor financial crime, had uncovered a conspiracy of staggering proportions. Now, they were racing against time to expose Thorne's plan before it could unfold in its entirety, to prevent a global catastrophe of unparalleled magnitude.

Their next move was a delicate dance of international intrigue. They needed to work with Interpol, coordinating efforts across multiple agencies and navigating complex legal and political hurdles. This wasn't just about catching a criminal; it was about preventing global economic collapse. The pressure was immense, each decision carrying potentially catastrophic consequences. Dimitri's unique skills proved invaluable. His military background provided access to information and resources unavailable to civilian law enforcement. His intimate understanding of covert operations proved crucial in locating and securing key pieces of evidence, pieces that even the most sophisticated cyber intelligence couldn't uncover.

The close collaboration between Dimitri and Benjamin, the unspoken language of shared experience and trust, started to heal some of the wounds inflicted by their past conflict, however slowly. The investigation took them across continents, from the bustling financial centers of London and New York to the shadowy havens of offshore tax havens. They found themselves in high-stakes negotiations with foreign governments, dealing with officials who were either complicit or deeply conflicted about exposing Thorne's influence. The closer they got to Thorne, the more perilous their situation became. Threats became more frequent, their movements tracked, their communications intercepted. They operated in a world of shadows, constantly looking over their shoulders, aware that they were being watched.

One of the most critical breakthroughs came from an unexpected source: a disgruntled employee of one of Thorne's shell corporations. This individual, fearing for his life, had secretly compiled a trove of incriminating data, detailing the intricate workings of Thorne's network. The data was encrypted, protected by multiple layers of security, but Dimitri's expertise in military grade encryption, combined with Cassie's ability to exploit human psychology and leverage weaknesses in the system, allowed them to crack the code.

The data revealed the full extent of Thorne's ambitions. It was a detailed blueprint of his plan, outlining the precise sequence of events he intended to trigger, the precise timing and methods he would use. It was a chilling testament to his meticulous planning and ruthlessness. It also revealed the identities of his accomplices, powerful figures operating within various governments and financial institutions who had been knowingly or unknowingly involved in his schemes.

Armed with this evidence, Cassie and Benjamin faced a new dilemma: how to expose Thorne without triggering the very chaos he sought to create? A sudden, public takedown could potentially send the global markets into a tailspin, far exceeding the damage already inflicted by Thorne's preliminary moves. They needed a more subtle, strategic approach, one that would neutralize Thorne without causing widespread panic. Their plan involved a carefully orchestrated series of simultaneous raids on Thorne's various assets a coordinated effort involving law enforcement agencies across multiple countries.

The operation was extremely sensitive and risky, demanding

flawless coordination and precise timing. One misstep could unleash catastrophic consequences. Cassie, with her innate negotiation skills, began to use her considerable leverage to sway key players. The information they had gathered was more than enough to bring down powerful individuals, not just Thorne. Using this leverage she carefully maneuvered through intricate political landscapes, securing support and collaboration from unexpected allies. She turned Thorne's allies against him by subtly suggesting that their continued complicity would lead to far greater repercussions if the investigation took a more public route.

The final confrontation took place not in a dramatic shootout, but in a quiet, secluded location, a place where Thorne had believed he was untouchable. Thorne, realizing his carefully crafted world was crumbling around him, attempted one last desperate gamble, a final, audacious attempt to trigger the cascading financial collapse he had meticulously planned. But Benjamin and Cassie were prepared. The climax was a tense showdown of wits, a battle of minds fought in the heart of the global financial system. It was a testament to their combined skills, a powerful blend of Cassie's keen intellect and strategic negotiation, and Benjamin's unwavering resolve and determination. Thorne's carefully constructed illusion shattered, he was left with no escape. The subsequent arrests sent shockwaves through the global financial community.

The exposure of Thorne's conspiracy, while causing initial tremors in the markets, ultimately led to a strengthened and more transparent financial system. The world had averted a crisis of unimaginable proportions, thanks to the unlikely alliance forged between a skilled negotiator, a determined detective, and a seasoned Navy SEAL. Though the scars of their past and the price of their victory remained, a sense of accomplishment settled over them.

The justice they sought had been served, and the world, for now, was safe. But the seeds of doubt and distrust had been sown; the future remained uncertain, a testament to the ever-present shadow of conspiracy and the constant vigilance required to protect the fragile balance of global stability.

CHAPTER 23

A Final Showdown

> "High above Monaco's glittering harbor, the opulent penthouse exuded an air of forbidden luxury. As Cassie, Benjamin, and Dimitri confronted Anton Volkov, the mastermind behind the conspiracy, the tension crackled with unspoken secrets. Their relentless pursuit of justice had led them to this climactic encounter, where the fates of powerful players and hidden machinations hung in the balance."

The opulent penthouse suite, perched atop a skyscraper overlooking the glittering Monaco harbor, pulsed with a tense silence. The air, thick with the scent of expensive perfume and the underlying tang of fear, crackled with anticipation. Cassie, her usually sharp attire replaced by something more practical – dark jeans, a close-fitting black top, and a concealed, but easily accessible, Glock – stood poised, her gaze fixed on the imposing figure pacing before the panoramic window. He was older than she'd expected, his silver hair impeccably styled, his tailored suit exuding an air of ruthless sophistication. This was Anton Volkov, the man who orchestrated the entire operation, the architect of the conspiracy that nearly brought the global financial system to its knees.

Benjamin, his usual sharp suit replaced by tactical gear, stood beside her, his hand resting lightly on the butt of his service weapon. He'd spent the last few weeks painstakingly piecing together Volkov's intricate network, using the information gleaned from the initial arrests and the interrogation of lesser players. The trail had led them here, to this seemingly impenetrable fortress, the final piece in the puzzle.

Dimitri, his twin brother, was positioned strategically at the perimeter, his team of SEALs securing the building, ensuring that this carefully orchestrated meeting wouldn't be interrupted. "You seem surprised, Detective Moore," Volkov said, his voice a low, cultured rumble that belied the ruthlessness in his eyes. He turned, a slow, deliberate movement, his gaze sweeping over Cassie and Benjamin. "I expected more…aggression." "We prefer efficiency," Benjamin replied, his voice calm but firm, betraying none of the tension he felt. "Less theatrics, more results."

Volkov chuckled, a dry, rasping sound. "Efficiency? My dear detective, you've spent weeks chasing shadows, wasting resources on a man who, I assure you, is merely a pawn in a far larger game." "You're the king, Anton," Cassie interjected, her voice cutting through the silence, clear and unwavering. "And your game is over." Volkov stopped pacing and turned his attention to Cassie. He studied her, a hint of amusement playing on his lips. "You're an intriguing woman, Ms. Holloway. I've admired your…tenacity. But you've underestimated me."

"We know about the offshore accounts," Benjamin stated, his voice steady and unwavering. "We know about the shell corporations. We know about the money laundering. We have enough evidence to put you away for life." Volkov shrugged, his nonchalance unsettling. "Evidence? My dear detective, you're dealing with a man who understands the intricacies of international law better than most of your colleagues. Your evidence is circumstantial at best. And even if it weren't, I have enough resources to ensure it never sees the light of day."

The atmosphere thickened, the silence punctuated only by the distant hum of the city below. The air crackled with unspoken threats, a silent battle of wills. Volkov's confidence was unsettling, but Benjamin knew it was a carefully constructed façade. He had seen the cracks in Volkov's composure during the earlier interrogations; the subtle flinches, the involuntary hesitations. He just needed to push him a little harder. "We have more than evidence, Anton," Cassie said, her voice low and dangerous. "We have witnesses. People who were directly involved, people who were scared into silence. People who are finally ready to talk."
Volkov's expression finally shifted, the mask of confidence momentarily slipping. A flicker of fear, barely perceptible, crossed his features before he quickly regained his composure. He took a sip of his expensive cognac, his hand trembling slightly as he raised the glass to his lips. "Bluff," he said, his voice strained. "A desperate attempt to salvage a failing case." Benjamin decided to change tactics. He pulled out a small, sealed envelope from his inside pocket, placing it carefully on the polished mahogany table. "We found this in your safe house," Benjamin said, his voice barely a whisper. " It contains a list of names – names of politicians, influential businessmen, even a few…judges. People you've been paying to ensure your silence, to ensure the success of your operations.

This, Anton, is not a bluff." Volkov's eyes widened, the color draining from his face. He stared at the envelope, his breath catching in his throat. The carefully crafted facade of composure crumbled, replaced by a stark, palpable fear. He knew, with chilling certainty, that the game was indeed over. The carefully constructed web he had spun for years was unraveling, thread by thread. The ensuing silence was deafening. Volkov stared at the envelope, his eyes darting nervously towards the window, then back to the envelope. His options were dwindling; his carefully constructed empire was crumbling around him. He knew that resistance was futile.

He looked up at Cassie and Benjamin, his eyes devoid of their former arrogance, filled with a desperate plea. "What do you want?" he whispered, his voice barely audible above the city's distant hum. Cassie and Benjamin exchanged a look. They knew this wasn't about revenge; it was about justice. It was about dismantling the network, exposing the corruption, and ensuring that no one else would fall victim to Volkov's schemes. This was a negotiation, but not the kind Cassie usually handled. This was a matter of bringing down a criminal empire. "Cooperation," Benjamin said, his voice firm but measured. "Full disclosure. You tell us everything, and we'll see that you get a fair trial. Refuse, and we'll make sure everything you've ever done comes to light, Anton. The choice is yours."

The weight of the moment hung heavy in the air. The city lights shimmered outside, a stark contrast to the grim reality unfolding in the opulent penthouse. Volkov's shoulders slumped. The fight had gone out of him. He knew he had lost. He was defeated, not by force, but by the relentless pursuit of justice. He nodded slowly, a single tear tracing a path down his cheek. The final act of this intricate game had begun. The dismantling of Anton Volkov's criminal empire had commenced. The long, arduous journey of bringing justice to those affected by his crimes was about to start. The ensuing hours were a blur of confessions, detailed accounts of complex financial transactions, and the meticulous unraveling of a vast criminal enterprise.

Volkov, under the watchful eyes of Dimitri and his team, revealed the names of accomplices, the locations of hidden assets, the intricate mechanisms of his money-laundering operations. His cooperation was thorough, driven by a desperate need to mitigate the inevitable consequences of his actions. Every detail he provided was carefully documented, each piece of information meticulously verified and cross-referenced.

As dawn broke over Monaco, casting a pale golden light across the azure waters of the harbor, the final pieces of the puzzle were put in place. Volkov's empire had crumbled, its foundations shattered. The intricate web of deceit and corruption was unwound, revealing a tangled tapestry of lies and betrayals. Justice had been served, but the scars remained, etched deeply into the lives of those affected by Volkov's reign of terror. The victory was hard-earned, but the feeling of accomplishment was profound. The world was safer now, the fragile balance restored, albeit temporarily. The shadow of conspiracy remained, a chilling reminder of the ever-present threat to global stability.

The battle had been won, but the war against injustice was far from over. The seeds of distrust, once sown, were difficult to eradicate. And for Cassie, Benjamin, and Dimitri, their journey was far from its conclusion. New threats would emerge, new conspiracies would unfold, requiring their unwavering vigilance, their unwavering pursuit of truth and justice. The uneasy alliance forged in the fires of this mission would be tested again and again, proving that their resilience, their loyalty to each other, and their unwavering commitment to justice was the only weapon powerful enough to combat the forces of darkness.

Their partnership, hardened in the crucible of this conflict, was a testament to the enduring human spirit, and a promise that they would be ready for whatever the future held.

CHAPTER 24

Unexpected Sacrifices

"Under the harsh Monaco sun, the black helicopter carried Volkov away, but the true battle was only beginning. As Cassie, Benjamin, and Dimitri stood on the tarmac, the weight of their recent triumph mingled with the daunting realization that the shadowy network of deceit extended far beyond their grasp. Their relentless pursuit of justice had only just begun."

The Monaco sun, harsh and unforgiving, beat down on the tarmac as a black helicopter lifted off, carrying Volkov away to a fate far worse than death. The sense of relief was palpable, but it was short-lived, replaced by a chilling awareness of the sacrifices made to reach this point. Cassie stood beside Benjamin, the salty air stinging her eyes, the events of the past seventy-two hours replaying in a dizzying montage.

The final confrontation with Volkov hadn't been a clean fight, a Hollywood-style showdown. It had been a brutal, drawn-out negotiation, a chess match played with lives as pawns. Volkov, even in defeat, remained a dangerous man, clinging to every sliver of leverage, every chance to escape. He'd used his knowledge of Benjamin's brother, Dimitri a Navy SEAL currently deployed in the Middle East, as a bargaining chip, threatening to release compromising information about a classified mission if they didn't play by his rules. The threat hung heavy in the air, a constant reminder of the precarious balance they were navigating.

Dimitri's involvement wasn't just a threat; it was a vulnerability. Cassie knew that Benjamin was grappling with a profound internal conflict, torn between his unwavering loyalty to his brother and his commitment to bringing Volkov to justice. He'd spent hours on the phone, coordinating with Dimitri's superior officers, desperately trying to minimize the risks without compromising the mission. The pressure was immense, squeezing the air from his lungs. His normally sharp features were etched with fatigue and concern. The weight of his brother's life, the fate of a top-secret operation, and the potential for international repercussions all rested on his shoulders.

The solution had been grim, a calculated risk that involved a carefully orchestrated deception. They'd leaked false information to Volkov, making him believe he had a
powerful ally within the intelligence community—an ally who was prepared to offer him protection and a new identity in exchange for his cooperation. The "ally" was a phantom, a ghost created by Benjamin and Cassie through a carefully orchestrated disinformation campaign that involved manipulating multiple intelligence agencies and planting false leads. This deception was incredibly risky, potentially unleashing chaos if exposed, but it was the only way to safely apprehend Volkov and neutralize his network without jeopardizing Dimitri's mission or exposing sensitive operational details.

This elaborate subterfuge hadn't been without its cost. A deep cover agent within Volkov's organization, a woman named Anya Petrova, who had been instrumental in gathering vital intelligence, had been sacrificed. Anya, a formidable operative in her own right, had been used as bait, willingly walking into the lion's den, knowing the immense risks involved. Her sacrifice, though clandestine, allowed them to pinpoint Volkov's location, his network's weaknesses, and ultimately, his capture. There was a profound silence, a shared grief hanging heavy in the air between Cassie and Benjamin, for a woman they knew only through her actions, but whose courage they could not deny. Her bravery underscored the often-unseen sacrifices required in the silent war against global terrorism.

The helicopter's departure was followed by a tense silence, broken only by the gentle lapping of waves against the shore. The realization dawned on them that the events in Monaco were merely a chapter, a single battle in a much larger war. Volkov's network was vast, his tentacles reaching into every corner of the globe. His downfall had only exposed the tip of the iceberg. The shadowy organizations he collaborated with, the corrupt officials he'd bribed, and the countless individuals who had profited from his criminal activities were still at large.

Benjamin looked towards the horizon, his eyes reflecting the vastness of the task ahead. He mentioned something about a meeting with his superiors at the Interpol headquarters in Lyon. This meant more paperwork, more briefings, more analysis. But more than that, it represented the formal start to dismantling the larger criminal network Volkov had headed. The sheer scale of it weighed heavily on him. The Monaco operation was just a beginning, a step forward into a landscape of seemingly endless intrigue and danger.

Cassie, noticing the exhaustion etched on Benjamin's face, placed a reassuring hand on his arm. She knew that the psychological toll of this mission would linger, leaving an indelible mark on both of them. They had witnessed the true cost of fighting evil, the price paid by those who operated in the shadows, fighting a battle unseen by the world. This mission, while successful, was a grim reminder that even in victory, there are casualties. The weight of responsibility rested heavily upon their shoulders.

The journey back to London was surprisingly quiet. Both Cassie and Benjamin were exhausted, both physically and emotionally drained. The adrenaline that had propelled them through the past few days was gone, replaced by a profound sense of weariness. The quiet hum of the airplane engine was a stark contrast to the cacophony of events that had unfolded in Monaco. The silence was broken only by the occasional sigh or a murmured word, as each struggled to process the events that had unfolded. Their silence, however, was not a sign of coldness or detachment, but a testament to the unspoken bond that had formed between them.

A bond forged in the crucible of danger, shaped by shared trauma, and strengthened by mutual respect. As the plane descended towards Heathrow Airport, Cassie looked out at the sprawling cityscape below, a vast landscape of lights and shadows. The city, like the world itself, was a complex tapestry of interwoven stories, some visible and some hidden, some bright and some dark. And they, Cassie and Benjamin, were part of this intricate web, protectors and players in the ongoing game of international espionage. The shadows they fought against were vast, powerful, and deeply entrenched, but they were also determined, relentless, and driven by a burning desire for justice.

The days following their return to London were a blur of debriefings, reports, and endless meetings. The details of the Volkov operation were painstakingly documented, analyzed, and disseminated throughout the relevant agencies. Cassie, a master of her craft, carefully navigated the bureaucratic maze, ensuring that all the loose ends were tied up and that the legal processes were followed. Her sharp mind and meticulous attention to detail were invaluable during these tedious yet crucial procedures. She worked tirelessly, her only reward the knowledge that she played a vital part in securing the world against a powerful criminal empire.

Benjamin, meanwhile, faced a different challenge: the aftermath of the operation's psychological toll. The sacrifice of Anya weighed heavily on his conscience, the knowledge that he had played a part in her ultimate demise a burden he carried silently. He found solace in his work, the routine of investigations offering a temporary reprieve from the darker thoughts that haunted his nights. The loss of Anya, however, prompted a deeper introspection into the ethics of their profession, the moral ambiguities of their work, and the inherent risks of their chosen path.

The tension between Benjamin and Dimitri, though eased by the successful conclusion of the Monaco mission, remained palpable. Dimitti's near-involvement in the operation served as a constant reminder of their vulnerability, a stark demonstration of the price they paid for protecting the world from unseen threats. Dimitri's return from the Middle East was greeted with both relief and concern. The unspoken understanding between the brothers, forged in the fires of adversity, held them together, but it was a bond strained and tested, perpetually vulnerable to the unpredictable currents of international espionage.

As the investigation into Volkov's network continued, new leads emerged, new players entered the scene, and the scope of the conspiracy continued to expand. The initial victory, though significant, only scratched the surface of a global criminal organization whose reach extended far beyond their initial expectations. The investigation revealed a network of corruption that spanned continents, involving politicians, businessmen, and even members of law enforcement. The uncovering of this conspiracy sent shockwaves through the international community, exposing the fragility of global security and the pervasive nature of organized crime.

In the quiet moments, Cassie and Benjamin reflected on the sacrifices they had made and witnessed. They were not merely detectives and negotiators; they were soldiers in a silent war, fighting against an enemy that operated in the shadows, using deceit, corruption, and violence to achieve their goals. Their commitment to justice was tested time and again, the moral dilemmas they faced demanding constant vigilance and courage. Their alliance, born from necessity, was strengthened by shared experiences, their trust deepening with each passing challenge.

The heart of the conspiracy, though seemingly exposed, had revealed a far more extensive and complex network, leaving them with the understanding that their journey was far from over. The war, it seemed, had only just begun. The seemingly resolved conflict in Monaco was merely the prologue to a far more extensive and dangerous chapter in their professional and personal lives.

CHAPTER 25

Victory at a Cost

"As the helicopter faded into the Monaco skyline, carrying Volkov away, a hollow victory settled over them. Beneath the surface of their fleeting triumph lurked deeper mysteries. Standing on the brink of an uncertain future, Cassie, Benjamin, and Dimitri sensed the shadows of a vast, elusive conspiracy, knowing their relentless quest for justice had merely uncovered the first layer of secrets yet to be revealed."

The helicopter's thrum faded into the background hum of the city as it disappeared into the azure sky. The Monaco coastline, usually a symbol of opulence and carefree living, felt stark and unforgiving. The victory, the capture of Volkov, felt hollow, a pyrrhic triumph achieved at a cost far greater than anyone anticipated. Benjamin stared out at the Mediterranean, the rhythmic crash of the waves a counterpoint to the turmoil within him. He'd seen death before, witnessed the brutality of violence firsthand, but this felt different. The weight of responsibility pressed down on him, a crushing burden. Cassie, sensing his turmoil, approached him, her hand resting lightly on his arm. "He's gone, Ben," she said softly, her voice a balm to his troubled spirit. "We did it." He nodded, but the words held no conviction. "At what cost, Cassie? At what cost?" The question hung in the air, unanswered, unspoken.

The cost was tallied in more than just the lives lost during the operation. It was measured in the subtle shifts in their alliance, in the unspoken anxieties that now hung between them like a persistent fog. The operation had exposed the fragile nature of their relationship, highlighting the precarious balance between their shared purpose and their inherent differences. Benjamin, a man of methodical investigation and unwavering adherence to procedure, and Cassie, a negotiator who often operated in the grey areas, their approaches to resolving the conflict often clashed. Now, standing on the precipice of a future shrouded in uncertainty, those differences threatened to fracture their partnership irrevocably.

Their success in Monaco had ripped away the carefully constructed facade of Volkov's operation, exposing a network far more intricate and dangerous than initially imagined. The documents recovered from Volkov's safe house were a Pandora's Box, revealing a labyrinthine web of corruption that stretched across continents, implicating individuals in positions of power and influence. The sheer scale of the conspiracy was staggering, a silent war waged beneath the veneer of civilization, a network fueled by greed, ambition, and a ruthless disregard for human life.

The faces of the fallen flashed before Benjamin's eyes: Sergeant Miller, a loyal, dedicated soldier who had given his life protecting the team; Agent Davies, whose experience and sharp wit had been instrumental in tracking Volkov; and the innocent civilians caught in the crossfire, victims of a conflict they never understood. Each face was a stark reminder of the human cost of their victory. The emotional toll was staggering; a silent grief settled over the team, a shared burden of loss that threatened to break them.

Cassie, despite her calm exterior, was equally affected. The weight of responsibility, the knowledge that lives were irretrievably lost due to this operation, had left its mark. She knew the risks inherent in her profession, yet this was different. The scale of the conspiracy, the callous disregard for human life, had shaken her to her core. The images of the chaos in Monaco, the sounds of gunfire and screams still echoed in her mind. She had witnessed the brutality firsthand; the vulnerability of life in the face of such calculated evil was a stark and sobering reality.

The immediate aftermath of the operation was a blur of debriefings, interrogations, and the painstaking process of piecing together the fragments of information gleaned from Volkov's safe house. The intelligence community was abuzz with the news; the capture of Volkov was a significant blow to the conspiracy, but it was only the beginning of the battle. The threat remained, lurking in the shadows, waiting for an opportune moment to strike again.

The next few weeks were consumed by a relentless cycle of work, each day a race against time to unravel the remaining threads of the conspiracy. The team worked tirelessly, sifting through mountains of data, analyzing financial records, and tracking down leads, their fatigue masked by a sense of grim determination. The global implications of the conspiracy were far-reaching, its tendrils extending into the highest echelons of power and influence. The stakes were higher than ever before, the risk of failure catastrophic.

Benjamin found solace in his work, burying himself in the details, seeking answers in the cold, hard facts. He
meticulously analyzed every piece of evidence, painstakingly reconstructing the network's intricate web of connections. The closer he got to understanding the conspiracy's full scope, the more terrifying it became. It was a network so vast and deeply rooted that it felt impossible to dismantle. The realization that this war was far from over, that the victory in Monaco was merely a fleeting moment in a much larger conflict, sent chills down his spine.

Cassie, ever the pragmatist, focused on consolidating their gains, solidifying alliances with other agencies, and ensuring that Volkov's confession was legally sound and airtight. She was well-aware of the dangers of exposing such a far reaching conspiracy; the risk of retaliation was significant. She understood the necessity of careful planning and strategic execution. The emotional cost of their victory weighed heavily on her, but she knew that wavering now would only invite further chaos.

One evening, after a particularly grueling session of analyzing intercepted communications, Benjamin found Cassie staring out the window of her hotel room, her silhouette outlined against the shimmering city lights. He walked over and stood beside her, the silence between them heavy with unspoken anxieties. "It's not over, is it?" she finally asked, her voice barely a whisper. Benjamin nodded, his gaze fixed on the city's twinkling skyline. "No, Cassie. It's far from over."

The gravity of their situation hung between them, a palpable tension that mirrored the perilous landscape they had to navigate. The victory in Monaco had been costly, a testament to the sacrifices made and the risks yet to come. The heart of the conspiracy remained elusive, its tendrils extending further and deeper than they could have ever imagined. The battle had only just begun. They had won a small victory, a brief respite, but the true war – the war for justice, for truth, and for their own survival – was far from concluded. Their alliance, tested and strained, would be pushed to its limits once again.

The journey ahead promised a relentless pursuit of justice, fraught with danger and uncertainty, demanding every ounce of their courage, skill, and unwavering commitment to the truth. The cost of victory had been high, but the fight for what was right was far from over. The chilling reality that their victory was only the first step in a much longer and more dangerous campaign settled upon them, a heavy blanket of foreboding. They knew, with a chilling certainty, that the shadows held more secrets, more dangers, and that the fight for justice was far from over.

CHAPTER 26

The Aftermath of the Crisis

"In the aftermath of the brutal firefight at the Radisson Blu, the scent of smoke and blood lingered in the air. As Cassie, Benjamin, and Dimitri surveyed the ruins, the chilling realization settled in: their hollow victory had merely peeled back the first layer of a vast, shadowy conspiracy. With each new revelation, the true scale of their adversary's reach became more sinister, demanding a relentless pursuit of justice in a world where trust was as fragile as life itself."

The air hung heavy with the scent of smoke and the metallic tang of blood. The once-immaculate lobby of the Radisson Blu lay in ruins, a testament to the brutal firefight that had just concluded. Shattered glass crunched underfoot, mingling with debris and the scattered remnants of hastily abandoned briefcases. The silence, broken only by the distant wail of sirens, was a stark contrast to the chaos that had reigned just hours before. Cassie, leaning against a scorched pillar, ran a hand through her disheveled hair, her usually sharp eyes clouded with a weariness that went beyond physical exhaustion. The adrenaline that had fueled her through the harrowing hostage rescue had finally ebbed, leaving behind a hollow ache.

Benjamin, his face grim and streaked with soot, stood beside her, his gaze sweeping across the scene. The weight of responsibility pressed heavily upon him; the lives saved, the lives lost, the lingering uncertainty of the true extent of the conspiracy's reach. His usually meticulous attire was now a mess of wrinkles and grime, mirroring the disorder in his mind. The events of the past few days had stretched him to his breaking point, blurring the lines between his professional life and the deep-seated familial conflict that had been reawakened.

His brother, Dimitri, a Navy SEAL whose tactical expertise had been instrumental in the operation, was already coordinating with the emergency services, his voice calm and authoritative amidst the controlled chaos. The contrast between Dimitri's composed demeanor and the raw exhaustion etched on Benjamin and Cassie's faces was stark. Dimitri trained to compartmentalize emotions, seemed unaffected by the gravity of the situation, his focus purely on damage assessment and securing the perimeter. The human cost of their victory was undeniable. Two hostages had been killed during the initial breach, and several others sustained injuries, their fates uncertain.

The perpetrators, however, had paid a heavy price. Three were dead, neutralized by Dimitri's precise marksmanship, the others apprehended, their stunned faces reflecting the sudden end of their meticulously planned operation. Yet, the sense of relief was tempered by a lingering unease. The conspiracy, though disrupted, felt far from dismantled. The true scale of their reach, the depth of their influence, remained largely unknown.

Cassie, her mind already racing, began to piece together the fragmented information they had gathered. The encrypted messages, the cryptic symbols, the seemingly random choice of target – everything pointed towards a larger, more sinister plot than they had initially imagined. The hostage crisis in London had been a carefully orchestrated distraction, a diversion designed to draw their attention away from the real objective. The question was: what was that objective? And how could they prevent it?

As the forensic teams began to sift through the wreckage, collecting evidence, Cassie and Benjamin found themselves alone amidst the ruins. The adrenaline-fueled intensity of the rescue mission had dissipated, replaced by a chilling realization of the vast, shadowy network they had uncovered. They had managed to thwart the immediate threat, but the victory felt hollow, the cost immense. The weight of unspoken questions hung between them, unspoken fears swirling in the silence. The intricate web of deception and betrayal they had navigated left its mark, a residue of mistrust and uncertainty.

The next few days were a blur of debriefings, interviews, and endless paperwork. The media frenzy was relentless, each news bulletin offering a new, often distorted, version of events. Cassie and Benjamin, exhausted but resolute, faced the relentless questioning, defending their actions, clarifying misconceptions, and trying to piece together the scattered fragments of the truth. The public hailed them as heroes, oblivious to the internal struggles, the doubts, and the lingering sense of betrayal that gnawed at them.

The betrayal, they realized, was not just from the external forces. Internal conflicts within their team mirrored the struggles of the external forces. The uneasy alliance forged under pressure was now under scrutiny. Trust, a fragile commodity in their line of work, had been tested to its limits. The emotional toll of the mission weighed heavily on them. The shared trauma had forged a bond, but the lingering mistrust from the betrayal of a trusted source created a subtle tension.

The investigation continued, peeling back layers of deception like an onion. Each revelation unveiled a deeper, more intricate level of the conspiracy. The network was wider and deeper than they had initially imagined. Its tentacles reached into governments, corporations, and even seemingly innocuous charitable organizations. The mastermind, or rather, the masterminds – for it turned out to be a group of highly skilled and sophisticated individuals –remained elusive, their identities carefully concealed. Their motivations remained shrouded in mystery, despite the substantial evidence collected.

Benjamin, grappling with his own internal turmoil, found solace in Dimitri's unwavering support. Dimitri, having witnessed the brutal reality of global conflict firsthand, understood the emotional toll on his brother and Cassie. He offered a pragmatic perspective, a grounding force amidst the emotional chaos. His insights, gained from his extensive military experience, were invaluable in analyzing the patterns of the conspirators' actions and anticipating their next moves.

The reconciliation between Cassie and Benjamin was not immediate, nor was it easy. Their contrasting styles and personalities still clashed, their methods often differing significantly. But the shared experience of near-death, the mutual respect for their skills, and the understanding that they were facing a threat that dwarfed individual differences slowly chipped away at their initial antagonism. They found common ground in their shared goal: to unravel the conspiracy and bring those responsible to justice. The unspoken understanding that their lives, intertwined by this mission, were now inextricably linked, strengthened their bond.

As they delved deeper into the conspiracy, they discovered an unexpected ally – a disillusioned former member of the organization. He provided crucial information, highlighting the vulnerabilities of the network and exposing the inner workings of the masterminds. This information was vital in forming their next strategy. He was a risky ally, his motives still unclear, his loyalty questionable, but in this high-stakes game of cat and mouse, even a shadowy figure could offer a helping hand.

The final confrontation was a tense, carefully orchestrated operation. The risks were immense, the stakes impossibly high. Using a combination of Cassie's negotiation skills, Benjamin's detective prowess, and Dimitri's tactical expertise, they managed to capture the remaining members of the conspiracy. The victory, however, came at a price. Dimitri was seriously injured, sustaining wounds that forced a long recovery. Cassie, though physically unharmed, bore the emotional scars of their shared trauma. They stood on the precipice of a new beginning, their relationship forever changed, their lives irreversibly marked by the events that had unfolded. Their partnership, initially forged in fire and mistrust, had evolved into something stronger, more profound.

The aftermath was far from peaceful. The global implications of the conspiracy were vast. Their actions had sent shockwaves through the political landscape, exposing the vulnerability of international institutions and the insidious reach of shadowy organizations. The healing process would be long and arduous, both personally and globally. But the seeds of a new beginning had been sown; a new alliance, a renewed understanding of trust, and a shared determination to expose and dismantle the deep-rooted corruption.

The fight was far from over, but Cassie and Benjamin, along with Mark, stood ready, their partnership hardened in the fires of this harrowing adventure. The final chapter was yet to be written, but the opening pages of their future collaborations were now inked, promising an exciting and dangerous journey ahead.

CHAPTER 27

Healing and Reconciliation

"In the aftermath of the Radisson Blu inferno, Cassie, Benjamin, and Dimitri faced the haunting echoes of their narrow escape. As they pieced together the shattered remnants of the conspiracy, each revelation drew them deeper into a labyrinth of deceit, where every step forward uncovered new layers of danger and uncertainty."

The acrid smell of burnt plastic and ozone lingered in Cassie's nostrils, a phantom reminder of the inferno they had barely escaped. She sat on a battered chair in the makeshift field hospital, the sterile scent of antiseptic doing little to mask the lingering stench of the Radisson Blu's destruction. Her body ached, a symphony of bruises and strained muscles, but the physical pain was secondary to the emotional toll.

The faces of the hostages, their terror and relief etched onto their faces, swam before her eyes. She'd witnessed too much death, too much suffering, in the past twenty-four hours. The weight of responsibility pressed down on her, heavy and suffocating.

Benjamin, his face pale but his eyes sharp and focused, entered the room. He carried a steaming mug, the aroma of strong coffee battling with the antiseptic. He sat down beside her, the silence comfortable between them, a shared understanding passing between them without words. Their uneasy alliance forged in the heart of a chaotic firefight was now solidified in a silent solidarity.

"Sleep?" he asked, his voice rough, the words carrying a concern that belied his gruff exterior. Cassie managed a weak smile. "Fitful at best. The screams..." she trailed off, unable to finish the sentence. The memory of the hostages' screams, the desperate pleas, the horrifying silence as the flames consumed parts of the building, were fresh wounds that refused to heal.

Benjamin nodded, understanding perfectly. "Mine too," he admitted, his gaze dropping to his hands. "I keep replaying it, trying to find something I could have done differently. Something to stop it all..."

"We did what we could," Cassie said softly, reaching out to cover his hand with hers. The contact was unexpectedly comforting, a silent acknowledgment of their shared trauma and the unwavering bond they forged in the face of extreme adversity. "We saved them, Ben. All of them. That's what matters."

He looked up, his eyes meeting hers, and a faint smile touched his lips. "Yeah," he agreed. "But it shouldn't have come to that. It shouldn't have happened at all."

They fell silent again, the unspoken questions hanging in the air like the smoke lingering in the destroyed lobby. The conspiracy that had almost cost them everything was far from resolved. The investigation was far from over. The true perpetrators were still at large. The ramifications would ripple through international politics and security for years to come.

The next few days were a blur of debriefings, interviews, and medical checks. Cassie and Benjamin, despite their exhaustion, found themselves working tirelessly, piecing together the shattered remnants of the case. Their collaborative efforts, surprisingly efficient, uncovered new layers of the conspiracy.

They painstakingly reconstructed the events of the hostage situation, analyzed security footage, and interviewed surviving hostages. Every detail, every clue, was scrutinized under the intense glare of their shared investigation.

Dimitri, Benjamin's twin, joined them, his military precision and tactical expertise proving invaluable. His presence was a welcome addition, a silent reassurance that they weren't alone in this fight. He was still grappling with his role in the near catastrophe, haunted by the possibility that his brother might have been killed. The guilt gnawed at him, and he found solace in working alongside his brother and Cassie, their shared commitment giving him a sense of purpose.

The process of reconciliation began slowly, subtly. It wasn't a grand gesture, but a series of small acts: shared meals, quiet conversations, the unspoken understanding that transcended words. Cassie, used to operating in isolation, allowed herself to lean on Benjamin and Dimitri, admitting her vulnerabilities. Benjamin, accustomed to a rigid stoicism, allowed his emotions to surface, revealing a depth of empathy Cassie hadn't expected. Mark, his usual jovial demeanor tempered by the trauma, found comfort in their shared companionship, a sense of belonging he hadn't expected in this shared mission and near death experience.

One evening, they gathered in a quiet corner of the secure facility, the city lights twinkling in the distance. The atmosphere was relaxed, a marked contrast to the tension of the previous days. They talked, sharing their fears, their doubts, their hopes. They spoke about the moments that almost broke them, the moments that forged an unbreakable bond. They talked about the future, about what they had to do to keep the world safe from the insidious threat they faced.

"I still can't believe we made it through that," Dimitri finally said, breaking the comfortable silence. "It was…a miracle."

"Not a miracle," Benjamin corrected him gently. "It was skill, cooperation, and a hell of a lot of luck. But mostly it was you two

pulling each other through, and saving the day, just as much as we saved those people." His eyes met
Cassie's, a quiet understanding between them acknowledging a shared heroism, a sense of joint responsibility, in a shared experience.

Cassie nodded, "But it still feels like it's something we shared. Something beyond skill and training." "We saved each other," Dimitri said quietly, his voice thick with emotion. The realization of their shared experience and the profound impact it had on their lives, was slowly and steadily healing them all.

As the days turned into weeks, the physical and emotional wounds began to heal. The collaborative investigation led to several arrests, dismantling a small part of the vast criminal network. The long road to complete justice lay ahead, but they had made a start. Their shared experience, the crucible of their newfound alliance, had changed them all. They had learned to trust each other, to rely on each other's strengths, to appreciate each other's unique perspectives. The bond forged in the fires of the Radisson Blu was more than just a professional partnership; it was a brotherhood, a sisterhood, born out of shared peril and a shared victory.

They emerged from the aftermath stronger, wiser, and more determined than ever before, ready to face whatever challenges lay ahead, their future collaborations already inked in the blood, sweat, and tears of a shared harrowing experience. This wasn't the end, but a new beginning. A new chapter, filled with promise, danger, and the unwavering resolve of a team forged in fire.

CHAPTER 28

The Cost of Justice

"In the heart of their clandestine hideout, Cassie, Benjamin, and Dimitri found themselves at a crossroads. Each clue they uncovered led to a deeper, darker mystery, where the lines between ally and enemy blurred. As they pressed on, the shadows of the conspiracy loomed ever larger, testing their resolve and unity in ways they never imagined."

The sterile scent of the hospital was a stark contrast to the chaos they had left behind. Benjamin, his usually sharp eyes shadowed with fatigue, sat beside Cassie. The adrenaline had long since faded, replaced by a gnawing emptiness. The successful rescue of the hostages felt like a pyrrhic victory. The images of the burning building, the screams, the desperate pleas – they were etched into their minds, a haunting soundtrack to their waking hours. The physical wounds were healing, but the emotional scars were deeper, more pervasive. Sleep offered little respite; instead, it delivered nightmares – vivid replays of the harrowing events.

Cassie traced the faint scar on her arm, a memento of a shard of glass during the escape. It was a small injury compared to the wounds inflicted on the hostages, some of whom were still grappling with severe trauma. The weight of their suffering pressed heavily on her conscience. She found herself questioning the cost of their victory, the price they, and others, had paid for justice. Was it worth it? The question hung in the air, unspoken yet palpable.

Benjamin, ever the pragmatist, struggled with the aftermath in his own way. He was haunted by the near-misses, the moments where the situation could have spiraled into unimaginable tragedy. He replayed the tense negotiations in his mind, searching for flaws, for missed cues, for anything that could have been done differently. The pressure he had felt during the crisis, the responsibility for the lives of so many innocent people, had left him drained, emotionally depleted. He found himself drinking more than usual, the bitter taste of scotch a temporary anesthetic for his inner turmoil.

Their shared experience had forged a bond between them, but it had also created a chasm of understanding. They were both haunted by the ghosts of the Radisson Blu, but their ghosts manifested differently. Cassie wrestled with survivor's guilt, while Benjamin grappled with the crushing weight of his responsibility as a detective. The emotional distance between them grew, a silent acknowledgement of the wounds they carried.

Their shared trauma wasn't confined to the two of them. Dimitri Moore, Benjamin's twin brother, the Navy SEAL who had provided crucial tactical support during the operation, bore his own silent burden. Dimitri accustomed to the clear-cut morality of military operations, struggled to reconcile the brutal realities of the hostage situation with his ingrained sense of order. The blurred lines between justice and collateral damage left him questioning his role, his purpose. He found solace in the routine of his training, the familiar comfort of physical exertion a temporary balm for his emotional wounds. Yet, even the rigorous demands of his physical training couldn't fully erase the images seared into his memory.

The investigation extended far beyond the immediate aftermath of the Radisson Blu incident. The arrests they had made were just the tip of the iceberg, a small victory in a larger, more insidious war against a sprawling international criminal network. The trail had led them through a labyrinthine web of offshore accounts, coded messages, and shadowy figures operating in the murky underworld of global finance. The deeper they dug, the more they realized the enormity of the conspiracy, the far-reaching tentacles of the organization they had inadvertently stumbled upon.

The investigation stretched their resources to the limit, demanding long hours, countless interrogations, and meticulous analysis of evidence. The constant pressure took a toll on their personal lives, straining their relationships with family and friends. The sacrifices they made were often unseen, their dedication to justice demanding a toll on their personal well-being.

Cassie, despite her unwavering commitment to her work, found herself increasingly isolated. The intensity of the case had driven a wedge between her and her closest friends, leaving her feeling alone in her battle. She struggled to reconcile her professional life with her personal needs, a struggle exacerbated by the lingering trauma of the rescue mission.

Benjamin, too, faced the consequences of his relentless pursuit of justice. His obsession with the case strained his relationship with his family, leaving him feeling guilty and inadequate. The relentless pressure of the investigation blurred the line between his professional and personal lives, leaving him struggling to find balance. He started losing sleep, and the dark circles under his eyes became a constant reminder of his exhaustion and self-doubt. His usually impeccable attention to detail slipped, and the pressure weighed him down.

The weight of the investigation extended beyond their personal lives, stretching the resources of the law enforcement agencies involved. The investigation required international cooperation, placing enormous strain on already stretched budgets and resources. The global nature of the conspiracy demanded collaboration between various agencies, each with its own priorities and agendas.

Negotiating these complex bureaucratic hurdles proved a significant challenge, and navigating the political landscape proved even more difficult. The pursuit of justice had a profound impact on the lives of the hostages, many of whom suffered from PTSD and other psychological trauma. The authorities established a comprehensive support network to help them recover, but the long road to healing was fraught with challenges. The psychological toll of the event rippled outward, affecting their families and communities.

The economic cost of the investigation was equally staggering. The investigation involved enormous expenses –from the deployment of specialized units to the analysis of complex financial data. The destruction of the Radisson Blu alone resulted in significant economic losses, disrupting businesses and causing widespread disruption. The city itself bore the scars of the event, both physically and economically.

As the investigation progressed, the lines between justice and vengeance began to blur. The relentless pursuit of the criminals involved pushed Cassie and Benjamin to the limits of their endurance, challenging their moral compasses. The temptation to take shortcuts, to bend the rules, became increasingly strong. The struggle to maintain their integrity in the face of overwhelming pressure tested their resolve.

In the end, their quest for justice was tempered by a profound understanding of its true cost. The victory felt hollow, a bittersweet triumph achieved at a high price, leaving them to grapple with the personal and emotional scars left in its wake. The aftermath of the Radisson Blu rescue was more than just a successful operation; it was a lesson in the complexities of justice, the sacrifices required, and the enduring burden carried by those who dared to pursue it. The road ahead remained uncertain, but Cassie and Benjamin, now irrevocably bound together by their shared experience, continued on their path, forever marked by the cost of justice.

CHAPTER 29

New Alliances and Trust

"In the wake of their perilous mission, Cassie, Benjamin, and Dimitri found themselves at the brink of new discoveries. Each revelation peeled back another layer of the intricate conspiracy, drawing them deeper into a web of deception and danger. What lay ahead in the shadows? Who were the true masterminds behind the chaos? Their bond, forged in the crucible of shared trauma and unwavering resolve, would guide them as they sought answers in a world where every step uncovered new, unsettling questions."

The weight of the Radisson Blu operation pressed heavily on them, a shared burden forging an unlikely bond. Days bled into weeks, the hospital's sterile environment slowly giving way to the bustling energy of London. Benjamin, despite his outward stoicism, found himself relying on Cassie more than he'd ever admit. Her calm demeanor, her ability to dissect complex situations with laser-like focus, was a welcome counterpoint to his own turbulent emotions. He saw her not just as a skilled negotiator, but as a formidable partner, a kindred spirit forged in the crucible of that terrifying night.

Their individual recoveries were intertwined. Physical therapy sessions often found them side-by-side, the quiet companionship a silent testament to their shared trauma. They discussed the operation in hushed tones, dissecting their individual actions, analyzing where they could have improved, where they'd exceeded expectations. These post-mortems weren't about assigning blame; they were about learning, about refining their skills for the inevitable next mission. The unspoken understanding between them deepened with each conversation, each shared glance.

Meanwhile, Benjamin's twin brother, Dimitri, a Navy SEAL with a reputation for unwavering loyalty and ruthless efficiency, remained a crucial, if sometimes unpredictable, element. Initially distant and guarded, his interactions with Cassie evolved from cautious observation to grudging respect. He saw in her a resilience that mirrored his own, a steely determination that didn't flinch in the face of overwhelming odds. He recognized the strain on Benjamin, the unspoken burden of guilt and responsibility that weighed heavily on him. Dimitri, ever the protector, began to see Cassie not as a threat, but as an invaluable ally, someone who could help bear the weight his brother carried. Their alliance extended beyond the personal. Whispers of a larger conspiracy, a shadow organization pulling the strings behind the hostage situation, began to surface. Intelligence gleaned from surviving hostages, corroborated by fragmented data recovered from the charred remains of the Radisson Blu, pointed towards a network far more extensive and dangerous than they initially suspected. This wasn't just a random act of terror; it was a carefully orchestrated event, part of a larger game played on a global stage.

The investigation led them to unexpected allies. A disillusioned MI6 agent, haunted by his past failures, offered crucial intel in exchange for protection. A former Mossad operative, now living in self-imposed exile, provided a cryptic map detailing the organization's intricate network of financial transactions and hidden operatives. Each new contact, each piece of information, was like a carefully placed tile in a vast, intricate mosaic, slowly revealing the terrifying picture of a shadowy organization bent on global destabilization.

These new alliances, however, came with their own inherent risks. The MI6 agent, known only as "Falcon," harbored deep-seated resentments and a penchant for reckless abandon. His loyalty was questionable, his motivations shrouded in a haze of personal vendettas and a thirst for redemption. The Mossad operative, a woman named Dr. Anya Petrova, carried a burden of her own, a past shrouded in secrecy and betrayal. Trusting either of them felt like walking a tightrope over a chasm of uncertainty. Navigating this treacherous landscape required a delicate balance of negotiation and deception.

Cassie, with her innate ability to read people and discern truth from falsehood, became the linchpin of their operations. She crafted intricate strategies, using her sharp wit and calculated charm to extract information from reluctant sources, to manipulate events to their advantage. She was a master of the subtle dance of deception, capable of weaving a web of lies that ensnared her targets while simultaneously safeguarding their position. Her skills extended beyond simple negotiations; she was a strategist, a tactician, capable of outmaneuvering even the most cunning opponents.

Benjamin, with his meticulous attention to detail and his deep understanding of criminal psychology, provided the necessary grounding for Cassie's often audacious plans. He meticulously analyzed the information they gathered, identifying patterns and connections that others missed. His sharp intuition, honed by years of experience on the force, allowed him to anticipate their opponents' moves, to preemptively neutralize threats before they materialized. Their partnership was a seamless blend of intuition and intellect, of calculated risk and unwavering resolve.

Dimitri, with his military background and his deep understanding of covert operations, provided the crucial muscle. His experience in high-stakes situations, his familiarity with clandestine tactics and weaponry, transformed their fledgling operation into a credible force. He acted as their shield, their protector, ensuring their safety while they navigated the treacherous waters of international espionage. His loyalty, unwavering and absolute, formed the bedrock of their operations. But even his unwavering support was tested. He questioned Cassie's methods on several occasions, his SEAL training prioritizing direct action and minimal collateral damage over Cassie's more subtle and nuanced approach.

One particularly tense standoff occurred in a dimly lit, smoke-filled backroom of a Prague nightclub. Their target, a high-ranking member of the organization, was surrounded by heavily armed guards. Cassie had devised an elaborate plan involving a diversion, a fake hostage situation, and a series of carefully orchestrated misdirections. Dimitri, however, favored a more direct approach —a swift, brutal raid, guns blazing. The tension crackled in the air as they debated their options, the weight of lives hanging in the balance. Benjamin, caught between his brother's impulsive nature and Cassie's calculated precision, found himself mediating their disagreement, his role as the bridge between these disparate worlds becoming ever more critical.

Ultimately, Cassie's plan prevailed. It was a testament to her understanding of human psychology, her ability to manipulate circumstances to her advantage. The raid was clean, swift, and virtually bloodless, a victory that cemented her position as an indispensable member of their team. Dimitri, though initially resistant, grudgingly acknowledged the effectiveness of her strategy, his respect for her tactical acumen growing with each successful operation.

The successful operation in Prague provided them with a treasure trove of information, leading them closer to the heart of the conspiracy. They discovered the identity of the organization's leader, a shadowy figure known only as "The Architect," a brilliant strategist with a network of influence spanning continents. The stakes were higher than ever before, the threats more imminent. The realization that they were facing an enemy of such magnitude, an opponent with resources and influence that reached the highest echelons of power, sent shivers down their spines.

The battle was far from over; it had only just begun. The alliance they'd forged, initially born out of necessity, had transformed into something deeper, a bond of trust tempered by shared experiences and mutual respect. They learned to rely on each other's strengths, to compensate for each other's weaknesses. They learned the hard way that trust, like justice, came at a price, a price they were more than willing to pay to bring The Architect and his organization to justice. Their journey was far from over; the path ahead remained fraught with danger, but they were ready, their bond forged in the fires of adversity, stronger and more united than ever before.

The lingering scent of gunpowder and the echo of gunfire were reminders of the cost of their actions, but their shared experiences, their mutual reliance, and the promise of a brighter future helped them persevere amidst the darkness and uncertainty that lay ahead. The fight for justice was a long one, but with their new allies and their unwavering trust in each other, they were ready to face whatever challenges came their way.

AUTHOR BIOGRAPHY

Demantaze Moore, known by the alias Sherlock, is an accomplished author whose work captivates readers with its intricate plots and compelling characters. With six years of service in the Army, including two years in military intelligence and two years providing Convoy Security, Escort, and Quick Reactionary Force, Demantaze brings a wealth of real-world experience to his writing. After his military service, he transitioned to the security industry, further honing his skills in strategy and protection.

Drawing from his extensive background in both military and civilian security, Demantaze crafts narratives that are not only thrilling but also grounded in authentic detail. His stories invite readers to explore the complex interplay of duty, loyalty, and justice in a world fraught with hidden dangers and moral ambiguities.

When not writing, Demantaze enjoys exploring new cultures, engaging in spirited discussions on global politics, and continuously seeking out new challenges. His commitment to justice and keen understanding of human nature shine through in his work, making each novel a testament to his life's experiences and values.

ACKNOWLEDGMENTS

Writing a book is never a solitary journey, and I am deeply grateful to those who have supported and inspired me along the way.

First and foremost, I extend my heartfelt gratitude to my family and friends, whose unwavering support and encouragement have been invaluable. Your belief in me has been my driving force.

To my fellow soldiers and comrades from my time in the Army, thank you for your camaraderie, bravery, and the shared experiences that have profoundly shaped my understanding of duty and resilience. Your stories and sacrifices are the heartbeat of my writing.

I am also immensely grateful to my colleagues in the security industry. Your expertise, insights, and dedication to protecting others have enriched my narratives, adding layers of authenticity and depth to my characters and their journeys.

A special thanks to those who provided critical feedback and guidance during the writing process. Your constructive critiques and encouragement have been instrumental in refining this story.

To my partner and editor, Cassandra Connor, your unwavering support, keen editorial eye, and relentless dedication have been a cornerstone of this book. Your insight and guidance have brought clarity and precision to my work, and your belief in this project has been a source of inspiration.

Thank you all for being part of this journey. Together, we have crafted something truly special.ve been crucial in bringing this story to life.

EPILOGUE

The late afternoon sun cast long shadows across the Thames as Cassie and Benjamin stood on the Millennium Bridge, the city a symphony of distant sirens and hurried footsteps. The Radisson Blu incident, though seemingly concluded, left an unsettling echo in the silence between them. The arrest of several key players in The Architect's organization had been a significant victory, but the network's tendrils extended far beyond their immediate reach. They knew this wasn't the end; it was merely a prelude.

Benjamin, ever the pragmatist, shifted his weight from one foot to the other, the city's relentless energy a stark contrast to the quiet introspection he felt. "They got most of the visible players," he conceded, his voice a low rumble against the backdrop of the city's hum. "But we both know The Architect himself is still out there. And he'll be regrouping, planning his next move."

Cassie, leaning against the bridge's railing, gazed across the river. The setting sun painted the sky in hues of orange and purple, a breathtaking spectacle that felt strangely out of place against the backdrop of their grim reality. "We underestimated him," she admitted, her voice soft but firm. "He's clever, resourceful, and he operates on a global scale. This wasn't just a London operation; it was a carefully orchestrated piece of a much larger game."

Her words hung in the air, heavy with the unspoken weight of their shared experience. The near-fatal hostage situation, the betrayal, the harrowing escape – it had all served to forge an unbreakable bond between them. They had seen each other at their most vulnerable, their most resilient. They had faced death together and emerged, scarred but stronger. "His network is extensive," Benjamin added, his gaze sweeping across the cityscape. "We need to anticipate his next move, not react to it. We need intelligence, connections, leverage. We need to expand our reach." He paused, then met her gaze. "We need to build a team."

The idea hung between them, a silent challenge and a shared opportunity. Building a team wasn't just about assembling skilled operatives; it was about finding individuals they could trust implicitly, individuals who shared their commitment to justice and understood the high stakes involved. This was about creating a network to counter The Architect's network, a force that could dismantle his organization from within.

The following weeks were a whirlwind of activity. Benjamin, leveraging his connections within the Metropolitan Police, began assembling a team of specialists. He sought out individuals with expertise in cyber warfare, intelligence gathering, and tactical operations – people who operated in the shadows, people who understood the nuances of international espionage. Cassie, meanwhile, focused on building diplomatic ties, discreetly contacting her network of contacts around the globe, establishing lines of communication and gathering intelligence.

Their efforts were not without their challenges. The bureaucratic hurdles, the internal power struggles, and the ever-present risk of exposure tested their patience and resolve. The constant threat of betrayal loomed large, a shadow that danced at the edges of their every interaction. Trust, they learned, wasn't something that could be easily granted; it had to be earned, painstakingly, through shared sacrifices and unwavering loyalty.

One evening, amidst the flurry of meetings and debriefings, Benjamin received a cryptic message. It was from his twin brother, Dimitri, a Navy SEAL currently deployed overseas. The message was brief, encrypted, and contained a single line: "The Architect's next target: Project Nightingale. Contact immediately." Project Nightingale. The name sent a chill down Benjamin's spine. It was a classified research project, shrouded insecrecy, involving advanced bio-weapons technology. If The Architect gained access to this technology, the consequences would be catastrophic. This was a threat that transcended national boundaries, a danger that could destabilize global security.

The revelation deepened their sense of urgency. The game had escalated dramatically, moving from a local crime syndicate to a global threat. Their uneasy alliance had solidified into a partnership of necessity, a bond forged in the crucible of adversity. They were no longer just chasing a criminal; they were fighting to protect the world from a looming catastrophe. Cassie, ever the strategist, immediately began to analyze the information. "Nightingale," she murmured, her fingers tapping a rhythm on her desk. "It's highly classified. Access is strictly controlled. He's going to need inside help, someone with high-level clearance."

Benjamin nodded, his face grim. "He's always played the long game. This isn't a spontaneous attack; it's been planned for months, perhaps years." He thought of Dimitri, his brother, risking his life in the far corners of the world. The weight of familial loyalty added a new dimension to their mission. This was personal now.

Their investigation led them to a network of corrupt officials, scientists, and mercenaries, all connected to The Architect through a complex web of financial transactions and coded messages. They painstakingly pieced together the fragments of information, building a profile of the organization's structure, identifying its vulnerabilities, and anticipating its next move.

The chase took them from the bustling streets of London to the sun-drenched beaches of the Mediterranean, from the snow-capped mountains of the Alps to the neon-lit alleys of Hong Kong. Each location presented new challenges, new risks, new allies and enemies. They encountered betrayal, close calls, and unexpected alliances. They learned to trust their instincts, to rely on each other, to compensate for each other's weaknesses and amplify each other's strengths.

Their partnership evolved, shifting from an uneasy alliance to a deep, unwavering trust. They learned to anticipate each other's moves, to finish each other's sentences. They had become a seamless unit, their combined skills and experience a formidable force against a formidable enemy. They had faced the darkest corners of the world, confronted the deepest betrayals, and emerged stronger, more resolute, and more determined than ever.

The journey was far from over, but they were ready. They had built a team, a network of skilled operatives bound by a shared sense of purpose and unwavering loyalty. They had the intelligence, the resources, and, most importantly, the trust, to face whatever challenges lay ahead. The fight for justice, for global safety, was a long and dangerous one, but they were ready to face the music, their destinies intertwined, their partnership forged in the fires of adversity, their future adventures waiting just around the corner. The lingering taste of victory was bittersweet, knowing that The Architect remained elusive, a ghost in the machine, ever-present, ever-scheming, but they were better equipped now, prepared for what was to come.

The world was a dangerous place, but they were ready to meet its dangers head-on. The chase was far from over, but with each passing day, their resolve hardened, and their commitment to justice burned brighter than ever. The path ahead was uncertain, but they were ready. They were partners, friends, and fighters. Together, they would face the storm.

AFTERWORD

As you close the final chapter of this journey, I hope you have been as captivated by the tale as I was in writing it. This story is not just a product of imagination, but a reflection of the experiences, lessons, and people who have shaped my life.

Through the eyes of Cassie, Benjamin, and Dimitri, I have attempted to weave a narrative that explores the complexities of human nature, the intricacies of global conspiracies, and the unyielding pursuit of justice. These characters are a tribute to the brave men and women I have had the honor to serve alongside, whose courage and dedication inspire me daily.

The road to completing this book was paved with challenges and triumphs, much like the adventures within its pages. Each twist and turn in the plot mirrors the unpredictability of life, and each character's struggle reflects the resilience of the human spirit.

I extend my deepest gratitude to you, the reader, for embarking on this journey with me. Your support and engagement breathe life into these words and give meaning to my work. It is my hope that this story has not only entertained but also resonated with you on a deeper level, prompting reflection on the themes of loyalty, sacrifice, and the relentless quest for truth.

As I pen this afterword, I am reminded that the story is far from over. The characters may find their resolution on the pages, but their echoes will continue to reverberate in our imaginations. The quest for justice, the unraveling of secrets, and the forging of unbreakable bonds are universal themes that will persist as long as there are stories to tell.

Thank you for joining me on this adventure. May we meet again in the pages of another tale.

With gratitude, Demantaze Moore (alias Benjamin Moore)

BOOKS IN THIS SERIES

The Moore Boys

Prepare to embark on a rollercoaster of mystery and intrigue with "The Moore Boys." This series introduces twin brothers, Benjamin Andre Moore and Dimitri Moore, whose turbulent childhood in the foster care system forged them into resilient, determined heroes. Their past is a mosaic of trials and triumphs, leading them to become extraordinary individuals.

But they don't face these adventures alone. Alongside them is the indomitable Cassie Ann, a powerhouse of knowledge and skill. Together, they delve into the shadowy realms of law enforcement and covert operations, unraveling secrets that lurk in the darkest corners of society.

With each turn of the page, you'll be swept into a world where nothing is as it seems. The Moore boys and Cassie Ann possess a unique blend of talents—courage, intellect, and tenacity—that make them an unstoppable force. Their quests are packed with heart-pounding action, unexpected twists, and the relentless pursuit of justice.

Dive into "The Moore Boys" series and join them on a journey where every clue leads to more questions, and every victory comes at a price. The mysteries are deep, the stakes are high, and the adventure is just beginning. Hold on tight—this is going to be a ride you won't want to miss.

Thank you for choosing to explore this thrilling saga. Get ready for the adventure of a lifetime, or perhaps two, as you uncover the many secrets that await in "The Moore Boys."

City Of Sin

The Moore Boys: City of Sin transports you into a gripping adventure featuring identical twin brothers, Benjamin and Dimitri Moore, whose much-anticipated vacation takes an unexpected turn when they receive a call from Caribbean authorities. While lounging under the sun-kissed skies of tropical paradise, the brothers are summoned to assist in unraveling a perplexing case that has captivated local law enforcement.

Dr. Henry Brown, a well-respected dentist known for his gentle demeanor and dedicated service to the community, is at the center of this mystery. Dr. Brown's life took a dramatic turn when he married Maria Stone, a formidable figure in the oil industry and a beloved member of society. Maria's untimely death just two years into their marriage left a profound impact on the community and her family. Inheriting her valuable necklace, which has been rumored to hold significant meaning beyond its monetary worth, are Maria's daughters, Helen and Julia. This necklace is now the focus of Dr. Brown's cunning scheme, as he seeks to infiltrate the Stone family legacy and claim his stake in the lucrative estate.

Unbeknownst to the brothers, nearby is Cassie Ann, a captivating and enigmatic woman whose vacation is also filled with ulterior motives. With her agenda shrouded in secrecy, Cassie's actions may intertwine with the ongoing investigation, adding another layer of complexity to an intricate plot.

As the Moores dig deeper into this thrilling narrative's unfolding twists and turns, they will face unexpected challenges, unveiling hidden truths about love, greed, and the lengths one will go to secure their legacy. Prepare for an exhilarating ride through deception and discovery as the twins navigate this treacherous landscape, where not everything is as it seems.

High Stakes

Prepare yourself for another thrilling adventure with The Moore Boys in "High Stakes"! This time, they team up with their sister, Simmeon, a brilliant strategist and expert in marine warfare, bringing her specialized knowledge to the group. Returning to assist them is the steadfast Cassie Ann, whose resourcefulness and unwavering support are invaluable. Adding to their impressive lineup is the formidable Master Sergeant Wilson, a battle-hardened veteran now using his extensive skills to safeguard humanity in the civilian realm.

Yet, looming on the horizon is a menacing new threat from the enigmatic 2nd Rite, spearheaded by the crafty Victor Staza. His nefarious plans for world domination are intricately tied to the powerful legacy of the Stone sisters, Julia and Helen. As tensions rise and danger escalates, can The Moore Boys muster the courage and ingenuity to confront this formidable adversary and save the day? The stakes have never been higher, and this promises an unforgettable journey filled with suspense and excitement!

Fractured Realities

Detective Benjamin Andre Moore finds himself caught in a reality-shattering conflict when he discovers a mysterious Orb linked to chaotic anomalies in Atlanta. As the boundaries between dimensions blur, Benjamin and his team—his twin brother Dimitri, the gifted Helen Stoner, the tech-savvy Cassie, the resilient Simmeon Moore, and the strategic Master Sergeant Wilson—embark on a perilous journey to stabilize the Chronal Rift and save their world.

Guided by Helen's newfound ability to sense the fractures in reality, the team navigates a fragmented dimension filled with interdimensional beings and unpredictable landscapes. They face intense confrontations with entities determined to protect the

Rift, culminating in a final battle where Helen confronts a malevolent force that manipulates the chaos.

Their victory stabilizes the Rift, but it comes at a great personal cost. As the team returns to a subtly altered Atlanta, they grapple with the lingering effects of their mission and the profound realization of the fragility of reality. United by their experiences, they prepare for the ongoing struggle to protect their world from the unknown threats that lie ahead.

"Fractured Realities" is a thrilling, multi-dimensional adventure that explores themes of identity, resilience, and interconnectedness. It sets the stage for a continuing saga of courage and determination in the face of cosmic upheaval.

Shattered Worlds

The story begins with Detective Benjamin Andre Moore receiving an urgent call about unusual disturbances in Atlanta. The city is experiencing anomalies that warp reality, causing chaos and fear among its inhabitants. Benjamin, along with his team—Helen Stoner, Cassie, Dimitri, and Simmeon—investigates these anomalies, uncovering that they are the result of a malevolent entity known as The Weaver.

The Weaver aims to merge its chaotic dimension with Benjamin's world, threatening to destroy everything. The team races against time to understand the nature of these anomalies and devise a plan to stop The Weaver. They face numerous external and internal challenges as they navigate this treacherous journey.

Helen establishes an interdimensional research center to study the anomalies while Cassie develops new technologies to detect and neutralize them. Dimitri trains specialized units for anomaly containment, and Simmeon leads support groups for those affected by the chaos. Together, they work tirelessly to protect their city and each other.

The story's climax is when Benjamin and his team confront The Weaver in a final, intense battle. They manage to destabilize The Weaver's power by overloading its energy nodes, ultimately destroying it. The vortex of chaos implodes, and the city begins to heal from the aftermath.

In the aftermath, the team faces the long-term consequences of their actions. They work on rebuilding the city and strengthening its defenses against future threats. They also unravel the mysteries of The Weaver's legacy, turning its remnants into opportunities for scientific advancement and protection.

As the story concludes, Benjamin and his team stand united, having faced their greatest challenge and emerged stronger. They are ready to embrace the future together, knowing their bond and determination will guide them through whatever comes next.

Detective Benjamin Andre Moore receives an urgent call about unusual disturbances in Atlanta. The city is experiencing anomalies that warp reality, causing chaos and fear among its inhabitants. Benjamin and his team—Helen Stoner, Cassie, Dimitri, and Simmeon—investigate these anomalies and uncover that they result from a malevolent entity known as The Weaver. The Weaver aims to merge its chaotic dimension with Benjamin's world, threatening to destroy everything. The team races against time to understand the nature of these anomalies and devise a plan to stop the Weaver. Throughout this treacherous journey, they face numerous external and internal challenges.

Helen establishes an interdimensional research center to study the anomalies while Cassie develops new technologies to detect and neutralize them. Dimitri trains specialized units for anomaly containment, and Simmeon leads support groups for those affected by the chaos. Together, they work tirelessly to protect their city and each other.

The story's climax features Benjamin and his team confronting The Weaver in a final, intense battle. They manage to destabilize

The Weaver's power by overloading its energy nodes, ultimately destroying it. The vortex of chaos implodes, and the city begins to heal from the aftermath.

In the aftermath, the team faces the long-term consequences of their actions. They work on rebuilding the city and strengthening its defenses against future threats. They also unravel the mysteries of The Weaver's legacy, transforming its remnants into opportunities for scientific advancement and protection.

As the story concludes, Benjamin and his team stand united, having faced their greatest challenge and emerged stronger. They are ready to embrace the future together, knowing their bond and determination will guide them through whatever comes next.

Echos Of The Rift

Echoes of the Rift follows a brave team led by Benjamin Moore as they navigate a world destabilized by the mysterious Chronal Rift. The story begins with the team stabilizing the immediate threat posed by the Weavers, an ancient and powerful group manipulating reality. However, their victory is short-lived as they realize the Weavers' power source must be destroyed to prevent future threats.

As they journey through a city haunted by shifting realities and anomalies, they confront Victor Staza, a former ally now aligned with the Weavers. The team battles to disrupt the Weavers' central point of control, risking their lives to protect their world. Despite the chaos, they manage to destabilize the core energy source, weakening the Weavers' grip on reality.

The epilogue sees the team standing on the edge of a new dawn, aware that their fight is far from over but united by their resolve to face future challenges together. Their journey symbolizes resilience, unity, and the relentless pursuit of truth in a world where reality itself is fluid and fragile.

Made in the USA
Middletown, DE
10 January 2025

68245869R00104